MURDER AT THE WEDDINGS

A ROSA REED MYSTERY BOOK 10

LEE STRAUSS
NORM STRAUSS

Copyright © 2021 by Lee Strauss

Cover by Stephen Novak, Illustrations by Amanda Sorenson

All rights reserved. No part of this book may be reproduced in any form or by any electronic or mechanical means, including information storage and retrieval systems, without written permission from the author, except for the use of brief quotations in a book review.

Library and Archives Canada Cataloguing in Publication

Title: Murder at the Weddings / Lee Strauss, Norm Strauss.

Names: Strauss, Lee (Novelist), author. | Strauss, Norm, author.

Description: Series statement: A Rosa Reed mystery ; 10 | "A 1950s cozy historical mystery".

Identifiers: Canadiana (print) 20220150338 | Canadiana (ebook) 20220150346 | ISBN 9781774092156 (hardcover) | ISBN 9781774092132 (softcover) | ISBN 9781774092149 (IngramSpark softcover) | ISBN 9781774092163 (Kindle) | ISBN 9781774092170 (EPUB) Classification: LCC PS8637.T739 M8749 2022 | DDC C813/.6—dc23

ROSA REED MYSTERIES

IN ORDER

Murder at High Tide
Murder on the Boardwalk
Murder at the Bomb Shelter
Murder on Location
Murder and Rock 'n' Roll
Murder at the Races
Murder at the Dude Ranch
Murder in London
Murder at the Fiesta
Murder at the Weddings

1

Things had a way of working out.

At least that was what Rosa Reed, secretly Mrs. Miguel Belmonte, liked to believe.

Despite many obstacles—forbidden love, lost love, love found again—Rosa had finally married the man of her dreams.

Rosa's happiness, however, didn't come without its challenges. Unfortunately, her new mother-in-law refused to accept her son's marriage status, which, naturally, had created all kinds of problems for Rosa and Miguel, the worst of which was not being able to live as husband and wife in the same house! Sure, they could defy Miguel's mother, but at what cost? A lifetime of familial strife? Rosa had convinced Miguel that it wasn't worth it. What was a month or two of inconvenience in exchange for a lifetime of peace?

The reason for Mrs. Belmonte's objection wasn't what Rosa had first presumed, that Rosa clearly wasn't Mexican. Rather, the real stickler was the fact that Rosa was not Catholic. Maria Belmonte, a widow, was fiercely protective of her family, and if their Latino culture was to be compromised, their religion would *not*. A Church of England wedding was no wedding at all!

Only a Catholic wedding would do, which was why Rosa, with Miguel by her side, was in the St. Francis rectory, sitting in Father Navarro's humble office and discussing their imminent second wedding.

"So nice to see you all again," Father Navarro said with a warm smile. The chairs had been arranged in a semicircle, facing him. He sat in front of his desk, making the meeting seem more like a group of friends getting together over a cup of coffee.

Along with Mrs. Belmonte, Miguel's sister Carlotta and his partner on the force, Bill Sanchez, were with them. Carlotta Belmonte, a first-time bride, seemed as nervous as an errant schoolgirl meeting with the headmaster. Likely because she had a bambino on the way, a secret that mustn't become widely known, at least until she was officially Mrs. Sanchez. Rosa smiled at her future sister-in-law, hoping to reassure her.

Smoothing out the satin folds of her A-line skirt, Rosa crossed her heels at the ankles. She'd chosen the pillbox hat that day, with its short veil resting on her forehead. She felt the style seemed more appropriate for the seriousness of the meeting, though the small combs that held it in place irritated her scalp.

Her physical discomfort was symbolic of the tension in the room, incongruous with what was meant to be a happy occasion occurring the next day. A double wedding! The idea had been Rosa's. Not only did it expedite Carlotta's big day, but a double wedding would also take the focus off Rosa and her shortcomings.

"Tomorrow is the big day," Father Navarro began. "Happily, we've received permission from the bishop for Rosa to marry in the church—" The priest smiled warmly at Rosa. "With such short notice, I feared . . ." He waved a fleshy palm. "But our God is a god of miracles, so we can rejoice."

Mrs. Belmonte, sitting straight, wearing a blouse and jacket, a pencil skirt, had her hands clasped on her lap, and a tight half smile on her face. She said, "Thank the Lord."

"I'll be glad when it's over," Bill Sanchez said. The burly detective had dressed in a crisp white shirt, blue tie, black trousers, and perfectly polished black leather shoes. His wiry black hair remained relatively untamed, the only outward clue to the "real" Bill Sanchez that Rosa had first met when she arrived in

Santa Bonita a year earlier. Carlotta Belmonte was responsible for revamping his usual unkempt appearance. Gone were the rumpled shirts, the ill-fitting and out-of-fashion trousers, and the faded shoes that looked like they had gone through a war. Rosa didn't doubt that he'd warm up to the family life he'd be experiencing by year's end.

He took Carlotta's hand. "Not only because I can't wait to start my life with my bride, but I don't like all the hoopla. Makes me nervous."

Father Navarro went through the agenda of the wedding ceremony to take place the next day—an extravaganza in Rosa's mind. One had to be made of hardy material to endure a Mexican wedding, which Rosa was told often went on for two days. She and Miguel had insisted that one day of celebration was long enough. Bill and Carlotta, eager to go on their honeymoon, had agreed.

Mrs. Belmonte had taken exception to the decision, her disgruntlement still riding one the surface. "A single-day celebration makes our family look cheap and inhospitable," she said with a huff. "But I always get outvoted."

Rosa couldn't stop herself from casting a look of incredulousness. This had been a rare instance where the woman had been overruled.

"Mama," Miguel started with strained patience,

"we're giving everyone double as it is, with two brides and two grooms."

Unplacated, Mrs. Belmonte blustered, "With all the rush, we hardly had time to organize anything longer, anyway."

Father Navarro cleared his throat, wisely changing the subject. "Miss Reed, it's my understanding that your parents will not be here to walk you down the aisle?"

"That's correct," Rosa said. "Sadly, my father's health won't permit the long journey." Rosa would've been troubled by her parents' absence at this wedding, except they *had* been at her *actual* wedding. Since the Mexican tradition was to have both parents walk their child down the aisle, Rosa had to come up with a replacement. "My cousin Clarence and my Aunt Louisa will walk me down."

The priest nodded. "That will do nicely."

"Unless—"

Rosa turned sharply to the familiar British voice coming from the opened doorway to the office.

"—Her brother walks her down."

Rosa sprang to her feet. "Scout! Oh my goodness." With American-style enthusiasm, Rosa ran to her adopted brother and gave him a warm embrace. "What a surprise!"

Scout smiled back. "How marvelous to see I pulled

it off." He leaned back and took Rosa in. "You look spectacular."

Scout was lithe and strong, and his diminutive size always gave him a look of youth, though Rosa noticed deepening lines around his eyes and a hairline that had crept upwards since she'd last seen him. "You look rather well yourself," Rosa said. Linking her arm through his, she brought him further into the room, where five sets of dark eyes stared back quizzically.

Rosa made introductions, leaving Miguel at the end. Scout reached out his hand in anticipation, and Miguel stood to accept it.

"You must be Miguel," he said. "Sorry I missed seeing you in London, old chap."

"It's a pleasure to meet you finally," Miguel returned warmly. "Rosa speaks of you often. Quite the horseman, I understand."

"It's a blessing to be able to spend time doing what one loves." Scout's blue eyes glanced at the five occupied chairs and the one left vacant by Rosa. "Do forgive me for interrupting your meeting. I was told I would find Rosa here, and I'm afraid my excitement overrode propriety."

"Nonsense," Rosa said. "We were just discussing details of the ceremony. And I believe you've just volunteered to walk me down the aisle."

Scout smiled his big toothy grin. "I do believe you're right."

Miguel pulled up an empty chair, and Scout took it. He leaned in with interest, and at times a look of awe, as Father Navarro told him all he needed to know.

2

Rosa sat with Scout on lounge chairs beside the kidney-shaped pool at the expansive Forrester mansion. The air was warm, and the patio lights shining off the pool made the water shimmer with rich blue luminescence. It was a perfect evening. Rosa wanted to pinch herself at the happy juxtaposition of seeing her very English brother here in the California town of Santa Bonita, overlooking the Pacific Ocean.

Scout was from a different time and place in her life. Thirteen years her senior, her brother had been away at boarding school or working at the horse races for most of her childhood. Her growing-up experience had been more like that of an only child. She and her brother hadn't grown up playing together, but her parents constantly spoke of him and were proud of his success as a jockey when he was younger, and now as a horse breeder. He'd set up stables on the family property known as Bray Manor, and cared for an older disabled cousin, Marvin, there, which was a testament to her adoptive brother's character.

Rosa had the vague knowledge that Scout had once lived as a homeless urchin, surviving on the streets of London before being adopted by her parents at the age of ten or eleven. Even as a child, Rosa had noticed a bit of cockney slipping into his speech, with a dropped *H* or a missing *G* when he got excited or tired. Sometimes he'd do it on purpose, to make her laugh, then roll his eyes at her and stick out his tongue.

What she remembered most was that Scout was always patient, kind, and protective of her and could make her giggle like no other. He had always brought her bonbons or Wrigleys chewing gum when visiting Hartigan House.

And this time was no different. He held out a small box he'd retrieved from his pocket.

"Scout?" Rosa said when she noticed it.

"It's for you."

"You didn't have to do that," Rosa said. "You being here is all the gift I need."

Scout laughed. "I couldn't very well come without a wedding present."

Rosa smiled in return. "I got the first gift, thank

you." Scout had sent them a fancy horse blanket, which Rosa had used to make a bed for Diego.

"Yes, how spoiled you are, getting a second wedding before I even get a first."

Rosa patted her brother's arm. "You've had plenty of chances. I don't blame a lady for not wanting to be put second to a horse."

Scout scratched his head. "I suppose that's true. I am rather single-minded."

Rosa lifted the lid of the box and gasped. Inside rested a pair of pearl-clustered earrings embellished with small gold leaves.

"All right, I confess," Scout said, "the present is actually from Mum. Apparently, they were once her mother's."

Rosa stared at the earrings. The only grandmother Rosa had ever known was Grandma Sally, who wasn't Rosa's blood relative. Sally Hartigan had been married to her mother's father, George Hartigan, and together, they'd had Aunt Louisa. Her mother's parents had died long before Rosa was born, and her father's when she was a young girl.

"They'll be perfect with my dress," Rosa said. "I feel like my family is properly represented with you and these stunning earrings here."

"You certainly have landed in a great spot here, Rosa." Scout leaned back on his lounge chair and closed his eyes. "A swimming pool. Tennis courts. And what is that I smell in the air? It reminds me a little of Italy."

Her brother had been stationed in Italy during the war. "Probably jasmine," she said.

"And it's warm so late in the evening." He sighed. "Splendid."

"Wait until you taste what the cook, Señora Gomez, has on the menu for our guests tonight. I think the long rehearsal has made everyone hungry. They'll be arriving soon."

"I've never had Mexican food before," Scout mused.

"Oh my, you are in for a treat. She's preparing her famous tortilla recipes for tonight." Rosa paused for a moment before lightly slapping her thigh. "I still can't believe you came. How incredibly kind of you."

"Well, I missed your first wedding to this Miguel chap, didn't I? Egypt was too far away for me to get back to London at short notice."

"It was rather unthoughtful of me, wasn't it?" Rosa said. "I hope you found some good horses, at any rate."

Scout whistled. "A couple of beauties."

Just then, Miguel and Bill Sanchez strode into the pool area, carrying two glasses of ale. Miguel offered his second one to Rosa, and Sanchez gave Scout the other before they took up two more chairs on the pool deck.

"I understand that congratulations are due for both of you chaps," Scout said, lifting his glass. "First-time double wedding for me."

"For us as well," Miguel said. "How was your journey?"

"I must say, this new mode of travel on an aeroplane was a bit disconcerting," Scout said.

Miguel nodded. "I found it the same when I went to London. I'm happy to keep my feet on solid ground."

"Flying into New York was something I had dreamed about for a long time," Scout added. "It was quite a sight from the air. But California? Let me just say that I understand the attraction."

"What kind of work do you do?" Bill Sanchez asked as he took a sip of his ale.

"I'm in the equestrian industry. I buy, sell, and breed horses."

"He was the one who taught me to ride," Rosa said cheerfully.

Scout grinned at her. "Now *that* is what I call being a good brother,"

Rosa's Aunt Louisa, followed by Rosa's two cousins, Clarence and Gloria, strode into the lamplight of the pool area, cocktails in hand. When Rosa had lived with the Forresters in the forties, her cousins had been children while she was a teenager. Rosa was pleased to get to know them now, as adults. Her aunt, somehow, had remained unchanged, a forceful personality to be reckoned with.

"Aunt Louisa loves to ride," Rosa said to Scout.

"Tremendous!" Scout sprang to his feet to shake everyone's hand. "It's a pleasure to see you all again."

A quick shared look of ill-ease passed between Scout and Rosa's American relatives. Rosa's failed first attempt at marriage, to Lord Winston Eveleigh, was the last time they'd all been together. Winston was at the altar waiting, with all the guests seated in the ancient stone church, when her father, Basil, had given her a final chance to back out. Rosa had taken it, humiliating her former fiancé—in fairness, and in retrospect, it turned out he deserved it—and bewildering all the guests. Rosa had felt bad that so much effort and expense had been incurred to get her American family to England. Still, despite the aborted ceremony, they had reassured her that they'd enjoy London immensely.

"I do hope we can ride together while I'm here, Aunt Louisa," Scout said with a smile. "I would love to see the countryside from the saddle of a good chestnut mare."

"Careful, Scout," Rosa cautioned. "In one sentence, you have just won the heart of our famous—

or is it infamous—" she raised a teasing brow, "Aunt Louisa. Something others can only aspire to. You might never be permitted to leave now."

Gloria and Clarence laughed a little too loudly, tapping their glasses together, and Rosa suspected those weren't their first drinks.

"I'm always happy to ride," Aunt Louisa said, though her eyes lacked sparkle.

Rosa held in a grimace. Aunt Louisa looked at Scout the same way she looked at Miguel, with a sense of superiority and distaste. Scout, like Miguel, was a usurper to the upper class to which the Forresters, Hartigans, and Reeds belonged. The poor were meant to be assisted, not adopted, and foreigners from the south were best hired to work in kitchens and yards. Like her housekeeper, Señora Gomez, and Alicia Rodriguez, the new nanny for Clarence's young daughter, Julie, who was assisting the cook for the party.

Scout didn't miss his aunt's look of disdain as Rosa had hoped, but Diego, Rosa's adopted gray tabby cat, played his role of timely distraction well. He joined the group and brushed himself along Scout's leg. Scout broke into his native cockney accent.

"'Ere now. What's this furry little fella up to then?"

The cat jumped blithely onto his lap, forcing Scout to hold his drink high.

"Diego!" Rosa scolded.

"It's all right. 'E knows a good man when 'e sees one, eh?" Scout put his drink on the table and lifted Diego with both hands. To Rosa's amazement, Diego purred as he bunted his forehead against Scout's nose. Two former street orphans saying hello.

"You have a way with animals," Rosa said happily.

Aunt Louisa pivoted on her heel, making an excuse to check on Señora Gomez in the kitchen, leaving a waft of self-importance in her wake.

3

When the buffet table was ready, most guests had arrived. It was conceived as an "after rehearsal" get-together where all those involved in the ceremony could meet each other. But there were also a few other guests there that were friends of the Forrester family; some Rosa had not yet met. Miguel and Carlotta's family were represented by their brothers, Hector, Mario, Ignacio, and their wives, and Maria Belmonte, who looked rather shell-shocked as she took in the opulent surroundings.

The Belmonte family came from "the other side of the tracks," with the humbler Belmonte home squarely in the Hispanic neighborhood. Whereas Aunt Louisa was snobbish regarding the lower classes, Mrs. Belmonte did the same with those from more fortunate circumstances. Her mother-in-law wasn't normally in a perpetually foul mood, but Rosa watched the woman's frown lines deepen as she noted all the staff at the Forrester mansion had brown skin and black hair.

Rosa sighed. She was helpless when it came to that. But at least Aunt Louisa paid fairly and treated the help well. Not everyone who worked in service could say that about their employer.

The thing about living in a small town—and compared with London, Santa Bonita was very small—was that everyone knew everybody, and when a celebration like a marriage took place, one couldn't get away without inviting everyone. Especially when one of the couples was related to the Forresters, a prestigious town family, and the other from a growing immigrant community.

As a result, many of Miguel and Bill's colleagues from the police department were present, along with Aunt Louisa's "good friend," a handsome older man named Elliot Roundtree. Wearing a nicely pressed western-style shirt with a bolo tie, the rancher looked more like he belonged to the Belmontes' guest list than to the Forresters'. Like Scout, Mr. Roundtree was an equestrian expert, though he enjoyed the western style, and it was through a shared love of horses and riding that her aunt and the ranch manager had become friendly.

A more-than-friends type of friendly. Yet, in

public, her aunt held Mr. Roundtree at arm's length, fearing word of her liaison with someone not part of her rich and powerful circle would get out. Aunt Louisa had high standards and was keenly aware of her hypocrisy. Rosa wished her aunt could lay her pride aside and allow herself happiness. One only lived once, and Rosa feared Mr. Roundtree's patience would wear thin.

If food was a social glue, tonight would be a great success. Señora Gomez, along with other Forrester mansion staff, had prepared a veritable feast featuring tortilla bowls and choices of brown rice with lime and cilantro, *ropa vieja* shredded beef, fiesta salsa shredded chicken, three levels of spicy roasted salsa, *pico de gallo*, pinto beans, and a whole separate table filled with different dips and desserts.

The four buffet tables had been set out on the large back patio of the Forrester mansion, and foldable chairs had been brought to accommodate the number of guests. Larger parties were held here during the warmer months. A record player played soft jazz in the background as the guests mingled around the tables.

"Good heavens," Scout said as he stared at all the food.

"Just stay away from the spicier stuff since this is your first time," Miguel advised, "and you'll be fine."

"And how will I know which is the spicy *stuff*?"

Miguel nudged Scout's shoulder. "I will be your guide, amigo,"

Minutes later, from across the crowded patio, Rosa watched as Scout took his first bite of food. To her amusement, she saw his eyebrows go up and his eyes widen. After enthusiastically chewing and swallowing his first mouthful, he jabbed his fork in the air and looked around as if to say, 'Is anyone tasting what I'm tasting here?' He then took another large mouthful, chewing more slowly this time, shaking his head in appreciation.

"The Englishman is gonna be okay, I think," Miguel said as he sat beside Rosa.

"Scout has always had a knack for adapting." Rosa watched her brother with affection. "He's spent time in the Middle East, so he has some experience with spicy food."

Miguel stared at his drink with a faraway look in his dark eyes.

"Is something wrong?" Rosa said, grabbing his hand.

"No, everything's going fine. I'm excited." Miguel lifted her hand and kissed it.

"But?" Rosa prompted. "I can tell something's bothering you."

Miguel let out a breath. "The entire Santa Bonita police department has been invited to the wedding."

"The police! Oh no, that will ruin everything," Rosa teased.

Miguel smiled, the dimples Rosa loved appearing as he did. "They always do."

"But surely, some must remain on duty?" Rosa said, with a twinge of concern. "Crime won't take a day off just because you're getting married."

"Straws were drawn," Miguel said. Adding with a grin, "the winners got to stay on the job."

"Rosa . . ." Aunt Louisa's voice reached them as she walked toward them, accompanied by a heavyset man in his early forties wearing a black business suit over a crisp white shirt and blue tie. He had a high forehead, wide brown eyes, and a round face. Aunt Louisa gestured between them. "Rosa, Miguel, I want you to meet Mr. Donald Sussman."

The man smiled warmly and reached out a beefy hand. "Pleasure's mine."

"Mr. Sussman serves on the advisory board at City Hall. He and I have advised the planning committee on several projects together over the last few years and have become friends. I hope you don't mind that I invited him to the wedding."

"Not at all," Rosa said.

"He has a son who married a lady from Argentina a few years ago, so I thought your wedding would interest him," Aunt Louisa said.

"Is that so?" Rosa said. "Do they live in Santa Bonita?"

Mr. Sussman shook his head. "Buenos Aires."

"Wow, that's . . ." Miguel began but was distracted by Alicia.

"I'm sorry, sir," she said. In her twenties, she had a shy smile, a thick Spanish accent, and a shapely figure that caught the eye of more than one man on the patio. "Mr. Belmonte, Señora Gomez sent me with a message for Mr. Sussman." Alicia kept her gaze down, glancing at Mr. Sussman for the briefest moment, but long enough for Rosa to catch a flash of emotion. Acting anxiously, Alicia seemed almost afraid of the man. Rosa could only wonder why. "He has a telephone call in the kitchen. They said it's urgent."

Mr. Sussman glared at Alicia, likely thinking her rude and inept, before excusing himself to take the call.

Rosa whispered to Miguel, "That was strange." She spotted Gloria at the pool's far end with her boyfriend, Jake Wilson, from *The Santa Bonita Morning Star*. They were chatting with an attractive young lady Rosa had yet to meet.

"Will you excuse me, love?" Rosa said to Miguel. "I want to meet Gloria's friend."

Miguel squeezed Rosa's hand before joining his family, who were huddled in a circle on the far side of the pool. Despite Rosa's desire to mix the families, it seemed everyone was determined to mingle with their own.

"Oh, Rosa," Gloria said when Rosa joined their small circle. "You must meet my friend Doris Brinkley." She linked arms with the young woman. "We met on set when I was working as an extra. You don't mind that I've asked her to join us?"

"Of course not," Rosa said. With this crowd size, what was one more?

Miss Brinkley was dressed in a fashionable capped-sleeve A-line dress. Her hair was dyed a glossy honey-blond and styled in a short bouffant.

"You're an actress?" Rosa asked.

"Yes." Miss Brinkley blushed. "Well, aspiring. There's a lot of competition, ya know."

"I'm sure there is," Rosa said. Acting had become one of the few ways for women to become wealthy in a short time, and Rosa didn't doubt many clamored for the chance.

"And you're the bride-to-be," Miss Brinkley stated. "How exciting."

"One of them," Rosa returned with a grin.

"I've already shown Doris my bridesmaid dress," Gloria said giddily, "and we were just wondering about your wedding dress." She clasped her hands in front of her like a schoolgirl.

"Hold the presses!" Jake Wilson quipped.

"Where's my notepad?" He made a show of patting his pockets.

Gloria pushed him playfully. "Go find one of mother's stuffed shirts to talk to." She pointed at Mr. Sussman. "That guy over there looks right up your alley."

Jake Wilson took his cue to move on from the fountain of girl talk that threatened to spill over, kissed Gloria on the cheek, and sauntered away.

Doris Brinkley wasted no time getting back to fashion. "Did you buy your dress in Santa Bonita? Chantel's on Main Street has some great dresses. They import too!"

"Actually, I brought it back from London."

Doris's jaw dropped. "London, England?"

Gloria grabbed Doris's arm. "Rosa's mother has a fancy dress shop there."

"So, what's the dress like?" Doris asked excitedly. "Come on, Rosa. Spill the beans."

"I don't know," Rosa hedged. "I'd like it to be a surprise for tomorrow."

"It's not the same one as last time?" Gloria said lightly, then quickly clapped a hand over her mouth.

"Last time?" Doris frowned at Rosa. "Are you a—" she whispered, "a *divorcee*?"

Rosa stared at Gloria, who looked back sheepishly.

"I was once engaged," Rosa explained coolly. "But

the ceremony wasn't completed." She was certain Gloria had been referring to her and Miguel's London wedding and not the failed engagement, but the diversion was necessary since her and Miguel's current married state was meant to be a secret. She didn't owe Doris a response, but to save Gloria's awkwardness with her friend, Rosa offered it. "You'll have to wait and see."

Gloria gushed, "Rosa, you're going to look beautiful!"

"Thank you," Rosa said. "Carlotta will as well."

Noticing Clarence sitting by himself, Rosa used her cousin as an excuse to leave Gloria and her forthright friend. At twenty-six, Clarence still had a boyish look. At first blush, one wouldn't guess he had already been married, divorced, and was the father of a five-year-old girl.

"I just spent time jawing with your brother," Clarence said once Rosa sat beside him. "Seems like a nice guy."

"He is. It's been so long since I've seen him. You're not terribly upset that he's going to walk me down the aisle instead of you?"

"Not at all," Clarence said before sipping his drink. "To be frank, I was nervous I might mess it up somehow. You know, trip on your veil or something."

Rosa laughed. "I'm sure you would've done a

wonderful job, but it would be nicer for you to watch it with Julie." Rosa glanced about. "Where is she, anyway?"

"Alicia put her to bed."

Julie must've fallen asleep quickly, as Alicia had returned to the party, helping Señora Gomez with the food. The nanny's gaze often flitted over to where Rosa and Clarence were seated, and Rosa hoped the young woman wasn't falling for her employer.

Rosa turned back to Clarence. "Vanessa's not having her this weekend?" Vanessa was Clarence's ex-wife. Their split had been acrimonious, but they'd found common ground for Julie's sake.

"Naw, she's got an out-of-town event, a party, or whatever. In any case, she's spending the weekend with her boyfriend."

Rosa raised her eyebrows.

"I know, I know," Clarence said with a wave of his hand. "But it works out since Julie is a flower girl at the wedding. I don't have to fight Vanessa about it."

New guests had joined the group. One tall, rather handsome man was accompanied by a platinum-blonde who seemed to have a Marilyn Monroe complex.

Charlene Winters, Miguel's former fiancée, had arrived.

4

No one would ever think of Rosa as a wallflower. Her parents were naturally attractive, and her mother had taught her grace and confidence, virtues that accentuated what one was born with.

However, when actress Charlene Winters entered the party—fashionably late—it was as if a spotlight had landed on her pretty head. Her curls were pinned around a round face, heavily made-up eyes, and bright red lipstick. And her curvaceous figure was draped in a form-fitting red polka-dotted pencil dress. She radiated Hollywood glamour. Had Aunt Louisa invited photographers, they would have been clamoring to take her picture.

Charlene Winters wasn't yet a household name,

but Rosa wouldn't have been surprised if that day came soon.

Rosa caught Carlotta glaring at the television star who had once been poised to be her sister-in-law. No bride wanted to be outshone by a female guest, and Rosa thought the term "guest" was generous on her part. Rosa felt for Carlotta as this wedding belonged to her, though Rosa didn't enjoy that the most beautiful woman at the party had nearly been Miguel's wife.

She took Miguel's hand and squeezed it. "Did you know she was coming here tonight?"

Miguel shook his head; his eyes were still focused on his former fiancée. Rosa squeezed his hand harder, and he broke his gaze.

"Sorry," he said. He wrapped a comforting arm around her shoulders. "It's just been so long since I've seen her."

He meant in real life, naturally. Charlene was a star of a popular television series, one that Rosa made sure they missed each week when it was scheduled. Thankfully, *Gunsmoke* played on a competing station at the same time.

"Who is she with?" Rosa asked. "Do you know him?"

Nodding, Miguel said, "That's Hank Brummel."

"That new officer from LA?" Rosa said. "He looks different out of uniform."

Miguel held Rosa's gaze. "We have to say hello," he said, "at least to Brummel. It would appear rude if we didn't, and—" he ducked his chin as he smiled. "I want to show off my beautiful wife."

"To be," Rosa added lightly. She needn't let Charlene Winters ruin this time between families. Best to be polite and get the encounter over with.

Miguel, leading Rosa by the hand, approached Hank Brummel. Charlene was chatting to someone behind Hank, who listened aptly and was clearly an admirer.

Mr. Brummel smiled a big toothy smile when he saw them and patted Miguel vigorously on the back.

"You dog! Puttin' on the ball and chain!"

Rosa's smile faltered, but she forced it to remain.

"Then again . . ." The man whistled as he took Rosa in. ". . . . she's a looker." He slapped Miguel again. "Congratulations, my man!"

"Thank you, Brummel," Miguel said. "I'm a lucky man. This is Rosa."

Hank Brummel took Rosa's hand and lifted it to his lips. "The pleasure's mine, darlin'."

Charlene Winters could hardly miss her companion's performance. She stepped in beside Hank, gave Rosa a cool look, then turned on her charm for Miguel.

"Miguel, darling, so good to see you again." She kissed him on the cheek, lingering in a fashion that made Rosa blush with embarrassment. Miguel had the good sense to step back.

"And you, Charlene," he said. "Congratulations on your success."

"Thank you!"

Instead of returning a sentiment of congratulations —she was at a wedding party, after all—she stroked Miguel's arm and giggled. "You must come to the set one day. We're filming in the desert just north of here."

"Only if there's a crime to solve," Miguel said jovially. "Work and my new wife keep me busy."

Charlene tilted her head coyly. "But you're not married yet."

Rosa had had enough of the woman's overt flirtation with her husband. There was a reason those who knew Charlene well referred to her as a floozy. Hank Brummel laughed heartily, as if he completely missed seeing that his date was flirting with the groom.

"My aunt needs us," Rosa said as a ruse. She'd had enough of Charlene Winters and felt her duty to greet her politely was well and done. "It's good of you to come." She tugged Miguel's hand and steered him away from Charlene and her oblivious date. Rosa hoped Sergeant Brummel's detective skills were better on the job than in Charlene Winters' presence.

After navigating Miguel to a group of policemen being entertained by Bill Sanchez, Rosa sought her friend Nancy. She was one of the few people that Rosa had kept in touch with that had been a part of her life when she went to school in Santa Bonita as a teen. Nancy had married her high-school sweetheart, and they had three sons who kept her busy. Rosa's life had taken a different turn, and they'd drifted apart, rarely seeing one another. Rosa was pleased Nancy had made it out that evening.

"You're finally getting your way," Nancy said, with a pat on her brunette curls. "After all this time." Nancy had witnessed Rosa, who, as a senior in high school had fallen in love with a brown-skinned soldier—a forbidden and ill-fated love affair. Aunt Louisa had been quick to drop the hammer when she'd learned of Rosa's attachment to Miguel, and had her on a ship to London as soon as she graduated.

"I am," Rosa said. "It's been a very long wait, but worth it."

Nancy lifted her cocktail glass as she gestured to the party underway poolside. "You're not going to miss living like this?"

It was understood that Rosa would move in with Miguel after the wedding. He lived in a quaint house near the middle of town. By quaint, Rosa meant the entire house was the size of the living room at the Forrester mansion. If it weren't for Mrs. Belmonte's refusal to acknowledge their English wedding, Rosa would already be happily living there.

"Sometimes simpler is better," Rosa said.

Nancy snorted. "That's easy to say, coming from someone who hasn't lived a simple day in her life. Imagine three rowdy boys, a busy and demanding husband, and not one single maid!"

Nancy grinned as she said it, but Rosa felt a sense of envy underneath the tease.

Her friend's eyes grew round, and she pointed past Rosa's shoulder. "Is that Charlene Winters? I watch her show. Wow, and she's here for your wedding?"

Rosa's jaw tightened. "She's the date of one of the police officers who works with Miguel."

"Wait!" Nancy's gaze dropped to the ground as her mind worked. "Didn't she and Miguel—" She stared at Rosa, then lowered her voice. "—date?"

"They did, but it's been over for a while," Rosa said stiffly. She couldn't help but follow Nancy's gaze to where Charlene—encircled by attentive men—giggled. Alicia, helping out by carrying a tray of drinks, strolled across the patio. Charlene excused herself from her group of male admirers and headed Alicia's way for what Rosa could only assume was a chance to exchange her empty glass for a full one. Alicia saw her coming and paused. But instead of stopping, Charlene plowed right into Alicia, causing the drinks to spill, and a number of glasses fell to the patio and broke.

"Silly girl," Charlene said. "You must watch where you're going!"

Alicia's eyes burned with tears as she scowled at the actress with indignation.

"Did you see that?" Nancy said.

Rosa nodded. "Yes." Charlene already had the attention of several men, but not the attention of the man she wanted. Rosa frowned. Had Charlene caused a scene with Alicia simply to get Miguel to respond?

"Excuse me, Nancy," Rosa said, leaving her friend to hurry to Alicia's rescue.

However, Clarence had reached his daughter's nanny before Rosa, or anyone else, could assist her. Clarence had never rushed to help someone clean up a mess before in his life, and Aunt Louisa stared at her son with contempt, clearly unhappy with his sudden impetus. Rosa gave her head a quick shake. Was her cousin about to make another bad relationship decision? And did he not care about the battle he'd be engaging in with his mother if he chose this girl?

But who was Rosa to judge? Many people believed she had done and was doing the same thing with Miguel.

Halfway between Nancy and Alicia, Rosa almost pivoted back but saw Mrs. Belmonte sitting alone. Her mother-in-law had made it clear on several occasions she thought Rosa's type was too hoity-toity for her family and worried that Miguel was in for a world of hurt by marrying her. Mrs. Belmonte being ignored by the Forrester side of the family certainly wasn't helping Rosa and Miguel's cause.

"Hello, Mrs. Belmonte," Rosa said cheerily. "Are you enjoying the party?"

Mrs. Belmonte's dark, gray-streaked hair was pulled back into a soft bun. She was the type who could light up a room with a smile one moment and darken it with a glare the next, a quality that could, and did, put the unsuspecting off balance. Presently, her expression was bland and non-committal. "It's . . . quiet," she said.

Rosa couldn't disagree. She'd been to a child's birthday party at the Belmontes' with music, chatting, and laughter that was so much louder and more boisterous than this. Pat Boone was presently playing on the record player brought outside for the occasion, and the music hardly stirred the emotions. However, it was easy to speak at normal volume over it, which Rosa appreciated.

"I suppose it is," Rosa said. "Tomorrow will be less quiet." The wedding reception had plenty of Mexican traditions planned. "The wedding will be exciting."

"Two for one," Mrs. Belmonte said, her dark eyes

unsmiling. "Carlotta and Miguel are my last to be married. I should have one more wedding left to plan and enjoy."

Rosa couldn't say much to that, except that she thought her mother-in-law was lucky to be seeing Miguel get married at all. Their British marriage was perfectly legal and binding in Britain and California.

Mrs. Belmonte's mood darkened, but at least she wasn't looking at Rosa. Someone else was responsible for her black look. Rosa turned to see what had soured Mrs. Belmonte's expression, only to feel her own facial features harden.

Charlene Winters again! Somehow, she'd cornered Miguel by the water fountain.

"She's a witch, that one," Mrs. Belmonte said. Her face softened when she looked back at Rosa, and Rosa felt a twinge of gratitude toward Charlene, as she seemed to be one person that her mother-in-law liked less than Rosa herself. "You'd better go," Mrs. Belmonte said, "before she casts a spell on our Miguel."

Rosa didn't believe in the superstitions of her mother-in-law, but she hurried to do what she was told. Was Charlene Winters going to be a thorn in her side forever?

The fountain was between Rosa and her husband, whom she assumed was held captive in the conversation he was engaged in. She dodged several people, promised to return for a chat in a moment, and reached the fountain in time to hear Miguel and Charlene mid-conversation.

"Micky," Charlene said, using Miguel's nickname in a way that made Rosa's stomach clench. "Don't marry her."

Rosa snorted. If Charlene only knew she was a month too late.

The actress continued her plea. "I know things got rough between us, but that was in the past. We have a future together, Mick, I know it!"

Mrs. Belmonte was right. Charlene was a witch!

Rosa leaned in, nervous at what Miguel was going to say. But she needn't have worried.

"I'm sorry you feel that way, Charlene," he said. "But I'm in love with Rosa—oh, hey, *Hank*."

Rosa wasn't the only one using the fountain as a shield to eavesdrop. Hank Brummel looked none too happy either. Rosa stepped into view, and the two couples glared at each other. Hank took Charlene's hand and roughly jerked her away, glancing over his shoulder with daggers cast Miguel's way.

"That went well," Miguel said snidely.

Rosa stretched up on her tiptoes and kissed Miguel on the cheek. "I'm in love with you too."

Miguel grinned and grabbed her tightly around the waist. "Let's just get this danged wedding over with,

Mrs. Belmonte." Then he kissed her with meaning on the lips. Too bad the fountain wasn't big enough to hide them from the view of all their guests! Rosa gently pushed her husband away. "Just one more night, darling. One more night."

5

Rosa had attended enough Catholic church services since her recent return from London to understand the church's theology and traditions. Still, she had to admit, she wasn't prepared for everything that made up a Mexican wedding mass—especially compared with the small, intimate English wedding she and Miguel had had three months before.

Rosa was with Carlotta in the vestry, along with a string of bridesmaids, including an excited and beautiful Gloria, and a gaggle of flower girls. Dressed in traditionally embroidered Mexican dresses, the little girls were under the guidance of Mrs. Belmonte.

"Girls! Girls!" the family matriarch cried. "You must be quiet and still. This is a house of God!"

Rosa glanced at Carlotta, who looked every bit like a nervous bride, a large bouquet in her trembling hands. She looked incredible in a thickly ruffled dress that looked like a white flamenco gown. She and her sisters-in-law had sewn it at the expense of the groom's family, another tradition new to Rosa.

Rosa reached for Carlotta's hand and squeezed it. "Are you all right?"

Carlotta's big brown eyes glistened. "I will be. I have so many emotions right now. Happiness, nerves, and—" she grimaced, "a little nausea. I'll ruin the whole wedding if I get sick on my way down the aisle."

Rosa laughed. "Please don't be sick." Rosa also had wedding nerves, but any anxiety she felt wasn't because of a growing little one inside her. Carlotta and Bill would have to endure suspicious speculation when their child arrived "early." But that was a problem for another day.

"Just breathe and keep your eyes on Bill, and everything will be fine," Rosa encouraged.

It had been decided that Miguel and Rosa would proceed down the aisle first, which in Rosa's opinion, meant that the spotlight would end on Carlotta and Bill, as it should.

Yellow California buttercups and purple daisies decorated the end of each pew, and the area around the altar had an abundance of candles. The late-morning sun sparkled through the abundance of stained-glass windows.

Even though Rosa's side of the family was far fewer than the Belmonte side, the pews on both sides of the aisle were filled. Perhaps this was because of Aunt Louisa's influence in Santa Bonita, but more likely, it was the extension of the Belmonte community. Either way, the church was filled with joyous expectancy.

Gloria, dressed in a pink chiffon A-line dress with full crinoline slips and a hemline that ended mid-calf, skipped to Rosa's side with glee on her face. "I've never been to a Mexican wedding before, or a Catholic one, for that matter. It's so exciting! I might just have to write a human interest piece on today's events." She ran a finger through the air as if underlining an imaginary headline. "English propriety marries Latin flamboyance."

Rosa wrinkled her forehead. "I certainly hope you don't!"

"Ah, Rosa, such a spoilsport. Tell you what, I'll give you veto powers."

"We'll talk about it later," Rosa said, "now get ready. It's about to begin."

Gloria squealed as she gave Rosa a hug. "Knock 'em dead, cousin!"

The organ began to play, and Gloria winked at Rosa before taking her first step.

The groomsmen were already waiting at the front, but, as per Mexican tradition, Miguel walked down the aisle with his mother and his brother Mario, who'd stepped in for their late father. They'd come from another room, but Rosa caught a glimpse of Miguel and Maria Belmonte as they approached the aisle. Her heart skipped as she soaked in Miguel's dapper appearance. He wore black dress pants and a traditional Mexican linen wedding shirt—with four small patch pockets and two rows of vertical, fine pleats—called a *guayabera*. Mrs. Belmonte had a stunned expression on her face that Rosa had seen on new actors with stage fright once they noticed everyone in the crowd looking at them. Poor dear.

"Are you ready?" Scout said as they waited at the end of the aisle. Like the Forrester men, her brother wore a fashionable suit with pressed trousers cuffed at the hem and resting on leather loafers. His white shirt was crisp, his thin black tie sharp, and his buttoned-down jacket fitted to perfection. Oiled to the side, his hair was cut short, especially around the ears. He looked very dapper, and Rosa couldn't be prouder.

"I am," Rosa answered. She smoothed out her dress, a fashionable white-satin number with a snug bodice and an A-line skirt blooming with crinoline, similar in style to her bridesmaids. It landed mid-calf, showing her white stockings and matching white-satin pumps. A short veil was pinned to her dark curls, and she wore her grandmother's earrings and a two-strand pearl necklace.

Scout's eyes flooded with affection as he looked at her. "You're stunning, Rosa. And they can be glad you're so good-natured, agreeing to do this. A lot of ladies would've refused and lived with the consequences."

Rosa shivered again, this time at the idea of such consequences. Giving up a day for exuberant celebration was a small price to keep Mrs. Belmonte on her good side.

The organ music paused and started again, indicating it was Rosa's turn. Scout gave her an encouraging look, and they started down the aisle.

As Rosa had anticipated, not everyone seemed to appreciate her modern dress or understand why her parents hadn't made the journey to walk her down the aisle, but there were plenty of smiles and even a few tears. Aunt Louisa, however, looked like she wanted to check her watch for the time, but Grandma Sally seemed happy to be doing something other than watching television. Nancy, who didn't look thrilled to be reminded of her own wedding, which had happened directly from high school, appeared to sigh. She glanced at her husband, who clearly didn't hide the fact that he was bored.

At least the Belmonte family faces looked

genuinely happy, even if Rosa's addition to their ranks was an oddity. Their joy for Carlotta and Bill was unconstrained.

After what felt like a seemingly endless walk, she approached the altar. Miguel's dark eyes locked on her as she stepped toward him, making her shiver. Rosa's knees felt weak under his serious, brooding, and passionate gaze. The intensity of their love made every inconvenience worth it. She'd marry Miguel Belmonte every day if need be.

Sandwiched between his parents, Bill Sanchez was next to make the trek. Like Miguel, he wore the traditional Mexican wedding garb. Watching from the front of the sanctuary, Rosa bit back a smile. The two men took up most of the space. It was a good thing Mrs. Sanchez was as slim as a wisp.

Finally, Carlotta presented herself, escorted by Mrs. Belmonte and Mario. Her extravagant dress and veil took attention away from her trembling bouquet. She kept her eyes on her groom, and after what seemed like an interminably long time to get down the long aisle, she was deposited at the altar by her mother and brother, who then took their seats in the front row.

Rosa's heart fluttered as Miguel took her hand, assisting her as they knelt on pillowy stools; Bill and Carlotta did the same. The priest began the wedding liturgy. Rosa was used to the mass performed on

Sundays and knew the wedding was an extra service before it, but she wasn't prepared for how long it would feel. She could only imagine Clarence propping his chin on his fist to avoid falling asleep. The little flower girls shuffled about in what must be growing, unimaginable boredom, and Rosa practically willed Father Navarro to hurry things along.

The brides and their grooms were provided chairs by each couple's *padrinos de lazos*, which translated to something like godparents.

Rosa smiled at her new relatives as they placed the *lazos*—linked together beaded necklaces—over Rosa and Miguel in a symbol of connected love and trust. The necklaces were light but weighted with meaning. Rosa held her husband's gaze, his dark eyes welling as he took her in. Souls destined to walk this earthly journey as one. Rosa shivered, surprised at how emotional she felt.

"It's now time for the *arras* ceremony," Father Navarro announced.

Miguel and Bill both reached into a trouser pocket, and each produced a small velvet bag. The men handed their respective brides a bag. Rosa already knew what was inside—thirteen coins representing Christ and his apostles, symbolizing the groom's intention to provide for the family, and the bride's confidence and trust he would do so.

Rosa's spirit of independence bucked against this last symbol, but instead of letting it make her feel like she was subservient to her husband, she chose to view it as a natural desire for Miguel to succeed in everything he did.

The exchange of rings followed. Rosa and Miguel shared a knowing look of déjà vu as they exchanged the same rings they had exchanged in London at their first wedding ceremony.

Next came the Presentation of the bouquet. Each couple, first Rosa and Miguel, then Bill and Carlotta, walked to the vestibule and knelt before a large image of the Virgin Mary. As a protestant who placed Mary on a lower pedestal and not as someone to be prayed to, Rosa had to bite her cheek at this tradition. She mouthed along as the two couples recited a rehearsed prayer to ask that the Blessed Virgin would intercede on their behalf for all their requests for the rest of their lives. Rosa and Carlotta left their bouquets on a nearby table as a gift. Cameras flashed like a sudden lightning storm.

Finally, la callejoneada, the wedding parade. Bill and Carlotta took the lead as the two couples marched out of the church. A mariachi band waited outside and came to life as the guests streamed out of the church, throwing confetti rice at the newlyweds on their way by. The band struck their first note and played enthusiastically and loudly, signalling the wedding party to lead the dancing crowd. Miguel grinned widely at Rosa, who could feel her eyebrows arching high on her forehead. The spectacle was very non-British. What would people think? Rosa decided she couldn't care less and decided to enjoy parading through the streets of the Spanish quarter of Santa Bonita, which was festooned with overhanging strings of festive flags. With Miguel, life was an adventure!

At one point, Rosa looked back to see Aunt Louisa, Clarence, Gloria, and Scout calmly walking arm in arm amidst the chaos of twirling and whooping. She shouted over to Miguel's brother Mario, who had been snapping pictures almost nonstop, to ensure he got a picture of her family braving the cultural storm. She was sure her parents would get a kick out of that.

Rosa felt a sense of euphoria when the procession returned to the church's elaborately decorated reception hall—it was done!

"We're married!" she said, beaming at Miguel. "Both in God's eyes, and your mother's!"

Miguel kissed her as he spoke. "Double the blessing." Then with a subtle tickle he whispered wickedly, "And double the trouble, or should I say fun."

Rosa laughed. "You'll just have to wait for that."

Inside, dozens of white-linen-covered round tables

had place cards showing the seating arrangements, which the Belmonte women had carefully curated.

At one end of the room was a curtained stage; at the other was a long table in front of a dance floor, where the two wedding couples and members of their party would sit facing the crowd.

The delicious smell of tacos, tamales, pork carnitas, chiles rellenos, and countless other Mexican delicacies emanated from the connected kitchen, which could be accessed by a swinging door and a pass-through window. By the time Rosa got seated, she was hungry.

The hall became filled with excited chatter as people, awaiting the newlyweds' arrival, found their seats. Upon entering, Rosa, Miguel, Carlotta, and Bill received a standing ovation. Rosa squeezed Miguel's hand.

They were all married at last!

6

Seated at the table designated for the brides and their grooms, Rosa turned to Carlotta. "You did it!"

Carlotta beamed back. "*We* did it!" Lowering her voice, she added, "Bill and I can't thank you enough for letting us take over your day."

Rosa took her sister-in-law's hand. "You're welcome. You were doing us a favor. I wouldn't have it any other way."

The first round of food was brought out on large trolleys covered with metal trays and placed buffet-style at one end of the room. A bartender operated a bar in the corner.

"Hey, isn't that your band?" Bill Sanchez said to Miguel. He pointed to the stage where a group of musicians set up instruments in front of the thick red curtains.

Miguel nodded. "Yeah, they're going to play a little while without me, and then later, I'll join them when the dancing starts." He chuckled. "My ma wanted them to play mariachi, but that ain't happening."

Miguel's brother Hector spoke a long prayer in Spanish from a microphone in the middle of the dance floor. Rosa couldn't understand everything, but the last sentence was in English: "Bless this food, amen!"

A loud shout rose from the crowd, and people headed to the food tables.

"The bridal party will be served," Carlotta said as a reminder.

"As it should be," Bill returned with a happy smirk.

Scout took his seat at the far end of the table. "I'm still stuffed from last night!"

"Hey, *hermano*!" Mario Belmonte walked up to the wedding table with his characteristic grin. Mario was known as the Belmonte family comedian, a title that Rosa knew Miguel liked to refute as often as possible.

"Mario," Miguel returned. He stood and gave his brother a quick embrace.

"You finally did it!" Mario said, still grinning. "Welcome to the club of happily married Belmonte men. It took you a while, but . . ."

"We can't all get married when we're twelve like you did," Miguel quipped.

"Well, I hope God blesses you with many kids." He turned to his sister and kissed her on the cheek. "You too, Carlotta. Or should I say, Mrs. Sanchez?"

"Gracias, Mario," Carlotta said with a smile.

"Hey, Miguel!" Miguel's brother Ignacio shouted from across the room as he stood beside one of the food tables. "*Lo siento!* The achiote chicken is already gone! Ha, ha."

Maria Belmonte, walking past her mischievous son, slapped his arm while those standing nearby laughed.

A moment later, the first dish of the five-course meal was brought to the wedding table, and everyone immediately dug in.

As the meal went on, an almost continuous stream of people came by to congratulate both couples on a beautiful wedding. Many compliments were paid to Carlotta and Rosa on their wedding dresses. At first, Rosa answered politely, thanking everyone for their kindness, but soon realized she would never get her meal finished if she continued that way. Hence, she followed her husband's lead and eventually fell into the rhythm of simply nodding and smiling while chewing a mouthful of food.

At the far end of the hall, Rosa spotted Charlene Winters. She hated how her eyes always seemed to seek Charlene out, and she wasn't the only one looking. Charlene, with her platinum-blond hair styled in a "poodle" and wearing a glamorous green silk gown with a matching scarf trailing down a bare back, looked every bit the movie star. Doris Brinkley was with her, gesturing to show she was displeased. Charlene spun on her heel, leaving Miss Brinkley to glare after her, and as she crossed the room, Donald Sussman crossed from the other direction, purposefully bringing her to a stop. Words were exchanged with lips tightly pursed. Charlene stepped around the man, who Rosa knew had a propensity for brashness, and returned to her seat beside Hank Brummel. The jovial countenance Rosa had encountered at the rehearsal party was gone from the man. Rosa didn't understand why they were there. Charlene seemed to sour everyone who crossed her path, and Rosa felt a sense of pity. Everyone else was a welcome delight, and Rosa planned to focus on those guests for the rest of the celebration.

Finally, after several hours, the empty serving dishes were cleared away to make room for dessert. Mick and the Beat Boys, minus their main lead singer, got up onstage and struck up a song Rosa had often heard on the radio sung by a smooth-voiced Italian singer named Dean Martin.

One girl, one boy,

Some grief, some joy,
Memories are made of this . . .

"A good song for us, eh, Rosa?" Carlotta said with a laugh, then started loudly singing over the band, 'Two girls, two boys,' while swaying to the gentle rhythm of the song.

The two couples took the floor first, and after a couple of stanzas, the guests eager to dance joined them.

Rosa gazed up at her handsome husband. "I'm actually really happy we did this," she said. "We've had two very different, very beautiful weddings."

"Doubly blessed," Miguel said, then kissed her gently.

When the first dance ended, Miguel whispered into her ear. "I have a surprise for you." Then he jumped onto the stage.

As if choreographed, Scout took Rosa's arm and led her to the front of the stage as the rest of the guests glided off the floor.

Miguel stared down at Rosa and said, "This is a song I wrote for my beautiful wife."

Rosa's hand went to her heart as if that could hold in her emotions.

The band put down their instruments and gathered in a semicircle around one microphone while snapping their fingers to a slow beat. The crowd grew silent as the song started.

It was performed a cappella and in the style of the black doo-wop harmony groups that Rosa had heard on American radio, such as The Drifters and the Moonglows. It was a style of music that Rosa had always loved from the moment she had first heard it. She had mentioned that fact to Miguel several times. Obviously, he had noted it.

The voices came in with the rich harmonies of the tenor and bass lines, filling the melodic lines instruments normally would. Miguel's clear strong voice sang out:

> *Everyone said that it could never be*
> *A girl like you with a boy like me*
> *And though we were born in worlds far apart*
> *I know it was always meant to be . . .*
> *Rosa, you got me staring at the moon*
> *Like young lovers always do*
> *I'm so glad you're finally mine again*

Rosa couldn't stop the tears that gathered around her eyes. She and Miguel had almost missed their happily ever after, and now, here they were! And such a beautiful song written in her honor. She felt like she was floating on clouds.

The song ended, and Miguel jumped to the floor and took her into his arms.

"I love you, Rosa."

"I love you too, Miguel."

Someone shouted *"La Víbora de la Mar"* so the band picked up their instruments for The Sea Snake Dance. The crowd whooped and cheered. A line of people formed while both wedding couples stood on chairs opposite one another and formed an arch by joining hands. The people danced through, holding hands in a long line.

The band played on:

You gotta dance with me, Henry, while the music rolls on . . .

It took several songs, each one faster than the next, before someone finally broke the line, and the dance ended.

Rosa, laughing and a little arm weary, glanced over to the table where Charlene Winters had been sitting. She noticed she and Hank Brummel hadn't participated in the Sea Snake Dance. Hank Brummel sat alone at the table, looking disgruntled.

The band played quieter love songs and ballads, giving everyone a respite from the earlier boisterous atmosphere. Rosa enjoyed the relaxing mood as she watched her handsome husband singing onstage, the beautiful lights and streamers drifting from the ceiling, and the audience swaying gently in their seats.

After about another half hour, Rosa saw the serving staff rolling out large linen-covered stainless-steel trolleys, and dessert was finally about to be served. The band stopped playing, and Miguel started down the stairs and toward Rosa.

Then a woman screamed.

A moment later, pandemonium broke out across the hall. Rosa's detective instincts kicked in as she jumped up from the table and ran toward where the scream had come from. Miguel arrived at that exact moment. Next to one of the large serving trolleys, several serving staff were standing, their hands over their mouth.

The doors to the compartment underneath the trolley were half opened.

A woman's arm hung out.

Miguel opened the steel doors further. Rosa leaned in to get a look at the body with its neck bent unnaturally, and gasped at the lifeless form of Charlene Winters inside.

7

"Help me get her out!"

Miguel directed his instruction to one of the police officers there as a guest. After awkwardly maneuvering the dead weight onto the floor, Miguel lowered himself to one knee and pressed two fingers to Charlene's neck, in search of a pulse, which could only be a matter of procedure since Charlene lay crumpled on her side in a twisted heap. Her blond hair was heavily matted with tacky blood on the side of her head.

Rosa gaped at Miguel before mouthing, "*Por todos los santos.*"

Bill Sanchez took in the seriousness of the situation and yelled into the hall. "All officers here, now!" He and Miguel quickly moved chairs in the way to block easy viewing and access.

That didn't stop mayhem from breaking out.

Mrs. Belmonte was fit to be tied. "What happened? Why has the music stopped?"

Those who saw the bloody arm quickly spread the word to those who hadn't. Mothers rushed about to gather their children. "Juan! Olivia! Come to Mama!" The anxiety in their mothers' voices caused some to cry, and the children were corralled and hushed.

Other wives were demanding answers from their husbands, "Are we safe?"

The police in attendance pressed in on Miguel and Bill. Miguel instructed a few to watch the doors and keep everyone inside, then ordered an officer to call the precinct. "There's a payphone outside."

Rosa waved frantically at Dr. Philpott. Dr. Philpott was Santa Bonita's chief pathologist and the primary doctor on call for suspicious deaths. A round and soft man with a balding head and permanent smile, he didn't come across as a man who spent his time with the dead. The pathologist and his rotund wife watched like a couple of gray-haired groundhogs peeking out of a hole. When Dr. Philpott saw Rosa's arm in the air, he jumped up from the table in a flash.

"Dr. Philpott," Rosa said when the man had reached her. "I'm afraid we have a body."

"I see."

Rosa led him to Miguel and Bill, who were still

guarding the scene. "I've brought Dr. Philpott," she announced.

Miguel nodded and stepped aside. "She's come to a humiliating end."

"Dear me." The pathologist glanced around at the commotion continuing in the hall. "Perhaps we should move the body into the kitchen."

"Sanchez, let's move the trolley back into the kitchen hallway," Miguel said, then instructed four others to move Charlene's body out of sight.

Rosa agreed it was a good idea as already some guests were curious.

Once inside the kitchen area, Dr. Philpott took a closer look at the body. "Hey, isn't this that actress?" He stared at Miguel. "The one you used to be engaged—"

"Yes," Miguel said before the doctor could finish his sentence. "She came as a date of one of my co-workers."

Dr. Philpott shook his head. "Such a pretty thing. What a shame."

Rosa swallowed back her discomfort and straightened her shoulders. She had to switch mental gears. She was no longer one of the brides—she was now operating as an unofficial counsel to the Santa Bonita police department. She would perform her duties with the utmost professionalism, even if the deceased had once been her husband's fiancée.

"The body was discovered around six-thirty," Rosa said. She'd checked her watch when Miguel went on stage. "Just as Miguel and his band were playing."

"Fairly obvious cause of death," Dr. Philpott continued. "Blunt force trauma to the skull."

Rosa's gaze darted about the kitchen. "That means the murder weapon is probably still in the vicinity."

"I have two officers rounding up the catering staff," Bill said as he lit a cigarette.

Gloria was hardly discreet as she tried to peek through the swinging door. Rosa moved quickly to meet her.

"Gloria."

"Rosa?" Gloria's eyes sparkled with excitement. "Did I see what I thought I saw?"

Rosa nodded grimly. "That's it for this wedding, I'm afraid."

"Who is it?" Gloria's eyes were wide with curiosity, and she jostled to see past Rosa's body. For the first time, Rosa thought Gloria might've found her calling in journalism. "Did I see blond hair? Come on, tell me."

Mrs. Belmonte poked her head through the pass-through window. "Miguel? What is going on? You must tell me. This is your wedding day!"

"If I answer your question," Rosa said to Gloria,

knowing that the news would be announced in good time anyway, "will you calm my mother-in-law?"

Gloria grimaced. "You drive a hard bargain."

Rosa lowered her voice. "Charlene Winters."

"Unreal!"

Rosa had barely ushered Gloria out when Hank Brummel burst into the kitchen. "Is it Charlene? I can't find her anywhere."

Miguel stared at the officer. "Where have you been?"

Rosa was curious about this too. All officers had been called to attention, yet Officer Brummel hadn't heard before now?

"I was outside on the phone." He pushed his way past Miguel. A tablecloth had been placed over Charlene's body, but strands of her curly poodle hairdo stuck out of the top.

"No! Not Charlene!" Officer Brummel's jaw twitched. "Who did this, Belmonte?"

"We don't know anything yet," Miguel said. "I'm sorry."

Rosa watched the man's face carefully. As Charlene's date, and a rather possessive one at that, he would naturally be considered a prime suspect. Officer Brummel cupped his mouth with a large hand, his eyes glassy with shock.

A natural response to seeing the slain body of

someone he cared for, or was he feeling guilty about what he'd done?

"What's going on, Miguel?" Mario Belmonte pushed his way through the swinging door. As the head of the family, Rosa imagined he thought he needed to take it upon himself to get to the bottom of the disruption. "Everyone's getting anxious. Why'd the music stop?" He waved his hands, expressing his exasperation. "And shouldn't there be dess—" On glimpsing a body covered up on the floor, he stopped short. "Oh."

Rosa followed as Miguel took his brother's arm and led him back to the hall. "No need to get involved, Mario. Go back to the family."

Mario pivoted away wordlessly. Miguel pursed his lips, ran to the stage, and jumped on. Grabbing the mic, he said, "Attention, everyone!"

"What's going on, Miguel?" a man shouted, his voice slurring. "We wanna dance!"

"I'm afraid dancing is out of the question, Dwight. Unfortunately, there's been an accident."

Voices called out, "What? What happened?"

"All will be explained shortly," Miguel said. "Please, everyone, go back to your seats. No one is to leave until the police say so."

Groans and murmurs spread through the hall, and the man Rosa now knew as Dwight grumbled loudly.

"You mean we can't dance?"

Rosa blew air out of her cheeks as she took in the hall and all the people there, her eyes moving from face to face. Among all these many guests was a killer. *Who?*

And poor Carlotta. Rosa's sister-in-law leaned into Maria Belmonte and sobbed.

"*Madre de Dios,*" Carlotta's mother said, her dark eyes flashing with angry indignation. "Do people not understand there's a proper time and place for things? My Carlotta's dream wedding is ruined!"

Rosa had stood at the marriage altar three times, and only one event had gone smoothly. At least she had that memory, but like some of her American friends, she liked to say, "Dang it all." She pushed her storm of emotions aside as her police instincts kicked in. The first few moments were crucial.

Rosa ducked into the kitchen area, trying to imagine what had happened. An altercation happened in the hallway, and Charlene Winters was murdered. The killer selected a trolley from the storage room and stuffed Charlene into the trolley compartment to hide the body, perhaps not realizing that the trolley would be used for dessert.

Having been focused on Miguel and the band and not her surroundings, Rosa knew it would be up to the police to determine who had left the reception.

There was the chance that the killer had already

fled, but that only meant it was doubly important to make an immediate note of who was present and who was not, most notably those who knew the victim personally.

Rosa returned to the table where Aunt Louisa—who'd refused to bring a date—and Grandma Sally sat. Clarence leaned back in his chair and repeatedly glanced at his watch. If he'd had plans to leave early, they were kiboshed now. Alicia held Julie back, carefully distracting her with crayons and a coloring book, but looking dreadfully pale. It was rather stuffy in the hall, and Rosa wondered what the nanny would do when she heard someone had died.

Gloria had returned to her chair, but the one next to her, assigned to Jake Wilson, was empty. "Where's Jake?" Rosa asked. "Everyone is supposed to be seated."

Gloria had the sense to blush. "He's using the payphone to call the paper. The death of a famous actress is big news!"

Rosa glowered at Gloria, then sighed. It wasn't like Gloria was on the phone trying to get a scoop.

"Please get him, and then stay in your seats," Rosa said. "This is a difficult enough situation as it is."

Gloria hurried away, and Rosa sat in Gloria's chair as she waited.

"I can't say I'm surprised," Aunt Louisa said.

Rosa raised a brow. "What do you mean?"

"You know," Aunt Louisa said with a dismissive wave. "These people aren't as civilized as the rest of us."

Rosa gasped. The things that came out of her aunt's mouth often astonished Rosa, but to say such things at a time like this! She had to assume her aunt was in shock and couldn't be held accountable for what she said.

Rosa held her tongue and turned her back to her aunt. From that position, her view of the main entrance led from the hallway into the reception hall. A killer had left the room while the band played, but who? Had someone noticed, or was everyone as enthralled by Miguel's romantic performance as she was? She'd even spotted the kitchen staff lining up against the wall, to watch.

The kitchen was empty, with no one to witness the altercation between Charlene and her killer.

What had Charlene been doing in the kitchen anyway?

Rosa took in the room. Bill Sanchez was among the police officers guarding the body. Miguel was in a deep discussion with Father Navarro. Sitting by herself at a table at the far end of the hall, Doris Brinkley looked oddly perturbed, her face flush. She removed a mirrored compact from her purse and touched up her lipstick.

Aunt Louisa's friend Donald Sussman headed for an exit, only to be stopped by a uniformed police officer who had recently arrived. Rosa couldn't hear what was being said, but Mr. Sussman looked surprised and annoyed that he wasn't permitted to leave.

Gloria returned with Jake Wilson on her arm.

Rosa cast a disapproving look his way but left him alone. He'd be questioned by the police soon enough.

Miguel jumped onto the stage and grabbed the microphone. Tapping it to confirm it was still on, he said, "Ladies and gentlemen, as you already know, the party is over. Detective Sanchez, helped by Father Navarro and some officers, will lead you all to the church sanctuary until further notice. Once again, I want to stress that no one is allowed to leave the premises until we can get everyone's name and contact information. Thank you all for coming. Obviously, this isn't how we planned for the wedding to end, and I'm sorry for it."

Moans and half-hearted booing followed, but the seriousness of the situation seemed to register with even the most belligerent types, and Rosa was relieved to see that cooperation was reluctantly granted.

8

"The catering staff number six people and probably have no connection with Charlene," Miguel said, rubbing his chin. "I recognize pretty much all of them."

"Why is that?" Rosa asked.

"Mick and the Beat Boys have played a lot of parties in the Hispanic community over the last couple of years. The catering company is called Viva Mexicana, the only Mexican catering company in Santa Bonita."

Bill Sanchez folded his arms across his chest. "The best tacos! They have their own salsa recipe. The spices are a carefully guarded secret. I . . ." He stopped when he noticed Miguel's annoyed look. ". . . will make sure we interview all of them thoroughly." He finished with a nod and then took a drag on his cigarette.

"Someone might have witnessed an argument or other unusual occurrence," Rosa said. "The kitchen was a busy place this afternoon."

Miguel squeezed his eyes and rubbed his forehead as if a headache was coming on. Rosa understood, feeling the stress of the circumstances in much the same way.

Officer Richardson had arrived and was taking photos with his Busch Pressman camera. Rosa and the officer were acquainted. When she'd started consulting with the Santa Bonita Police, Officer Richardson had held some animosity toward her. She'd finally confronted him, and things had gone much smoother after.

"What was Charlene doing in the kitchen?" Miguel asked.

"She could've been lured in," Rosa suggested. "Nearly everyone was focusing in the other direction, on the stage. Or, she could've been followed."

"Why would Charlene go this way of her own volition?" Miguel asked. "Unless . . ."

"Unless?" Rosa prompted.

"There's a staff restroom at the back. It's not as nice as the public ones in the foyer, but it's private. Charlene liked to . . ." Miguel glanced away sheepishly, and Rosa understood he was about to share something intimate about another woman with his new wife.

"It's all right, Miguel," she said carefully. "It's a murder investigation now."

After a long breath, Miguel said, "She liked to spend a lot of time doing her makeup."

"Yeah, she liked to use a lot of paint, all right," Bill Sanchez said, blowing smoke. "Like Salvador Dalí or something."

Rosa and Miguel shot Bill a look. For a moment, Rosa had forgotten he was standing in hearing distance.

"What do you know about Dalí?" Miguel said to him.

"Mexican guy. Painted a lot."

Miguel rolled his eyes. "He's Spanish, Sanchez."

"If you say so." Bill flicked his cigarette into a glass ashtray on a nearby table. "The point is, he was good with colors and took his time to do a good job."

Rosa stared blankly at Bill, then turned to Dr. Philpott. She hoped to pull the conversation back on track. "Any guesses as to the height of the assailant or the strength?" she asked. "Man or woman?"

"From the marks on the skull, I'd say she was approached from behind," Dr. Philpott said. "The impact looks as if the assailant wasn't too much taller than the victim but was strong enough to do the damage."

"It took some strength to put the body into the trolley," Rosa said. She'd been around enough dead bodies during her career as a police officer in London and her time as a private detective in Santa Bonita to understand the difficulty involved in moving dead weight.

Dr. Philpott agreed. "Miss Winters looks to weigh about one hundred and twenty-five pounds."

"A strong woman could've done it," Bill said, "but my bet's on a man." He stared at Miguel. "I hate to say it, but Brummel—"

"Not looking forward to it," Miguel started, "but we've gotta talk to him." He sighed, then continued, "Father Navarro said we can use his office to interview."

Bill inhaled and smoothed out his shirt. "I'll round him up."

"I'm going to look around in the kitchen," Rosa said.

Bill stopped short. "This is your wedding day! You can leave this to the police."

"He's got a point," Miguel said.

Rosa cocked her head and raised an eyebrow. "I'm going to remind both of you that it is your wedding day too."

"Yeah, but . . ." Miguel began.

"From the look in her eye," Bill said with a crooked grin, "I don't think you're gonna stop her, partner."

Rosa placed her hands on the waist of her white

wedding dress. At least she'd removed the veil before the reception. She hardened her look as she stared at the two detectives. "We're all investigators. We were all here on the scene when it happened. No one else is more qualified than the three of us to solve this murder. Wedding day or not. I'm certain Chief Delvecchio would agree, aren't you?"

"I booked off work for our honeymoon, Rosa," Miguel said, but his eyes moved to the body, once again hidden under the sheet. The ambulance attendants had arrived and were about to move the corpse to the morgue.

"We can honeymoon after the murder is solved," Rosa said consolingly. They'd already had a lovely honeymoon in France, and if it hadn't been for Charlene's death, Rosa would have had the relief of dropping the ruse of this wedding, honeymoon, and everything involved in what she considered a marriage deception. "It's Bill and Carlotta who need to go on a honeymoon."

"We had plans for Acapulco," Bill said. He stared at Miguel, his new brother-in-law, with doe-like eyes.

"You two should keep your plans," Miguel said with a sigh.

"You're sure?" Bill asked, a note of hope in his voice.

"Yes, but would you mind rounding up Brummel

first?" Miguel nodded toward the door. "Before I change my mind?"

"Yes, sir!" Bill said, then jogged away.

Miguel shouted after him, "And take your lovely bride home with you!" Then he ducked his chin and took Rosa's hand. "Are you sure you want to do this? It would be perfectly understandable if you sat this out."

Miguel's concern touched Rosa, but what on earth would she do with herself as she waited for her new husband to come home? They were finally meant to spend the night at his house . . . *their* house. There was no way she was going back to the Forrester mansion and acting like she was still an unmarried woman.

"I only want to be with you, Miguel, even if it means this," Rosa said. "Now, let's see if we can find the murder weapon."

Miguel's eyes sparkled. "You are an amazing woman, *Mrs. Belmonte*. I can't believe my good fortune." He took her hand and led her to the now-empty kitchen.

"Nor mine, *Mr.* Belmonte."

The seriousness of the situation tempered Rosa's giddiness. She could imagine the frustration and impatience of the guests, including her own and Miguel's family, who still waited in the church. Unfortunately, their disappointment and inconvenience couldn't be helped.

As if reading her mind, Miguel said, "I've got Edwards and Pike taking names and statements. Our families will be the first to be released." He shook his head. "I'd rather be searching for clues than dealing with my mother and brothers right now."

Rosa felt the same way.

The kitchen that serviced the church hall was built with large events in mind, with linoleum flooring, laminate countertops, and solid appliances.

When the trolley was rolled out, the staff had been cleaning the dinner dishes. Stacks of dirty plates and cutlery were piled on almost every spare counter space and several large trolleys just like the one that had contained the body of Charlene Winters.

The storage room where the trolleys were kept was in disarray as if certain trolleys had been quickly discarded. Rosa tested a couple and could confirm that they had a broken wheel. Perhaps that was why the waiter who pushed the trolley with the body's extra weight had failed to recognize it. He'd probably thought another wheel was giving out.

Rosa returned to the kitchen, taking in the evidence of chaotic meal delivery. A portable, top-loading dishwasher with the finished-cycle indicator on was incongruous with the dishes piled on the table.

Opening the door, Rosa saw it was empty except

for a single cast-iron frying pan of considerable size, now wet and sanitized.

9

"That is one big, heavy frying pan," Miguel observed after a long moment.

"That is one big, heavy, and terribly *clean* frying pan," Rosa corrected.

"Yep, that would do it, all right. But you would have to put your back into it. Not that easy."

"One would need strong hands and a tight grip," Rosa said.

Officer Richardson, one of the officers who had found themselves lucky to remain on duty instead of attending the wedding, stepped into the kitchen. "I'm finished taking photographs, Detective."

"Would you find Señora Morales for me?" Miguel replied.

Señora Morales was the staff manager of Viva Mexicana Catering, having taken over the position when her husband had passed away. "And bring the fingerprinting kit back with you."

"Sir."

Rosa glanced about the kitchen, then through the door and the adjoining hall into the trolley room. "What exactly happened here?" she mused aloud.

Returning to the hallway, Rosa started toward the exit door at the end but, passing a connecting hallway, pivoted quickly to see where it led. she found herself at the far end of the foyer in no time. This was the way to access the kitchen without going through the reception hall or entering from the back door.

She returned to the kitchen hallway and opened the exit door. As she had imagined, it led to a parking lot and the location of the trash bins. Back inside, just before the exit, two doors were opposite one another in the hall. The first one opened to the janitor's room. Shelves were crowded with cleaning solutions, towels, and bars of soap. A mop, bucket, and push broom were tucked away in the corner.

The door directly across from the janitor's room was a kitchen restroom outfitted for one. Although not nearly as nice as the public ones in the foyer, it was clean and provided privacy.

Had Charlene come here for that reason? Rosa found nothing on the sink's edge. She lifted her wedding dress skirt and ducked down. Near the wall was a tube of lipstick. Rosa unrolled a section of toilet paper and reached for the tube. Careful not to disturb the fingerprints, she opened it up. Bunchberry Red.

"Did you find something?"

Rosa stood at Miguel's voice and held out the lipstick tube. "I'm pretty sure this is Charlene's. A dusting for prints will confirm. It places Charlene here."

Miguel held out an evidence bag, and Rosa dropped the lipstick into it. "Got this from Richardson. He's in the back with Sofía Morales. He's dusting as we speak."

Sofía Morales was a heavyset woman in her early fifties, clothed appropriately in a white dress with a full-length apron, stained where she'd grabbed it to wipe her hands.

"This wedding was a big job," she said as she looked around the messy kitchen. "*Muy grande*. Two big wedding cakes, and many pies and flans! Many guests."

Sofía Morales struck Rosa as a capable woman who clearly had considerable cooking and management skills to direct multiple staff members at large events like this.

"Was the dishwasher running while you and your crew watched the band play?" Rosa asked.

"Oh no. It's too noisy. I'm told it was donated to the

church by a rich man, but *phff*, I think washing by hand is the best." Mrs. Morales set her gaze on Miguel, her face softening with affection. "I let the women watch your beautiful song, Detective Belmonte." Her eyes grew glassy with romantic notions. She placed her fingers on her lips, kissed them, then released them quickly like chefs do to describe a delicious meal. "*Muy bonita.*"

"I'm happy you enjoyed the song," Miguel said.

"*Si si!*" She grabbed Rosa's hand. "You are a very special lady."

"*Gracias*," Rosa said.

"And you were the first to return to the kitchen afterward?" Miguel asked.

"*Si* and this machine was going." She pointed at the dishwasher being dusted for prints by Officer Richardson. "I don't know who turn it on. I ask everyone!" She spread her hands in the air in front of her and shrugged her shoulders. "I see all my workers watching the music. No one come in here. I was standing near the swinging doors. I see everyone."

Thanks to Miguel's captivating performance, Sofía Morales had effectively given the entire kitchen staff an alibi.

"But there is another way into the kitchen," Rosa offered. "I saw a connecting hallway."

"Sí, but no one from Viva Mexicana go there. We use the back door to go in and out."

"Someone could have accessed the staff bathroom from that adjoining hallway, and you wouldn't have seen it, necessarily."

Sofía Morales pulled a face and nodded. "I suppose. We are very busy working in the kitchen. We don't pay attention to what goes on behind us."

"Thank you, Señora Morales," Miguel said. "You're free to go home."

"But . . ." The caterer waved an arm at the kitchen. "What about this mess? And what am I to do with all the leftover food?"

"As you can see," Miguel said, "the police are busy here. Someone will notify you when you can return."

Rosa waited for the woman to disappear into the reception hall, then turned to Miguel. "Charlene, then her assailant, must've entered the kitchen from that adjoining hallway. With the staff standing in the reception hall, the killer had easy access. Either Charlene finished in the restroom at an opportune time or was lured out. Perhaps an argument ensued, and the killer grabbed the frying pan from the kitchen counter and used it as a weapon."

Miguel took up the narrative. "Once the assailant realized Charlene was dead, he tossed the evidence into the dishwasher and turned it on."

After Miguel had secured the crime scene, instructing a couple of uniformed officers to keep watch, Rosa, Miguel, and Officer Richardson returned to the sanctuary. The flower decorations at the end of the pews were wilting, and the candles had all been snuffed out. A sense of sadness filled Rosa. It was hard to believe that a beautiful double wedding had taken place in this space only a few hours earlier. Now it was dotted with a few people sitting in pews being watched by Officers Edwards and Pike.

The one Rosa knew as Officer Pike approached when he saw them enter.

"Status?" Miguel said.

"Edwards and I got everyone's statements and addresses, and those we confirmed were in the room at the time of the killing could leave."

Rosa was pleased that the familiar faces of the Forrester family and the Belmonte family were nowhere in sight.

"Who's left?" Miguel asked.

"Hank Brummel." Officer Pike ducked his chin. "And he's none too pleased."

"We'll see to him first," Miguel said. "So, his wait will end shortly. Continue."

Officer Pike referred to a small notebook he held in his hand. "A Miss Doris Brinkley, Mr. Donald Sussman, and Miss Alicia Rodriguez."

Rosa's head shot up at the sound of the familiar name. "Alicia Rodriguez?" The name was common enough. Could there be two?

Rosa's hopes were dashed when Officer Pike cast a sheepish glance her way. "She says she works for your cousin, Mrs. Belmonte. Uh—" Another glance at his notes. "Mr. Clarence Forrester. As a nanny."

"That's right." Though they were standing at the back of the sanctuary, Rosa could, on closer inspection, recognize the back of the nanny's head. It was a mistake, surely.

The church door slammed open, and Rosa was startled to see Clarence storming in.

"Rosa! Thank goodness I found you," he said, looking flustered. "I'm told they're holding Alicia. That's bogus!"

"I'm certain it's a simple mistake," Rosa nodded. "Do you want to wait for her? We'll speak to her shortly and get things cleared up."

Clarence rubbed the back of his neck. "Yeah, all right." There was a bench in the foyer, and Clarence took long strides to it and sat.

"I really need to speak to Hank first," Miguel said once Clarence was out of earshot. "I'd say you could talk to Miss Rodriguez on your own, but I should be in on the interview."

"Of course," Rosa said. "A short wait won't hurt her."

As she followed Miguel to Father Navarro's office, Rosa glanced over her shoulder and saw Clarence staring morosely into his hands. A wait might not hurt Alicia, but Clarence could be a different story.

10

*I*n Father Navarro's office, Rosa sat on a folding chair close to the window, notepad in hand. Officer Hank Brummel sat on another. Miguel occupied the priest's chair on the other side of the desk. The tension was raw and awkward, with one man mourning the death of an ex-fiancée of the other.

Miguel clasped his hands and rested them on the desktop as he leaned in. "I'm sorry we have to do this, Hank, but of course, you understand the necessity."

Judging from Officer Brummel's red, swollen eyes, he was either fighting back his emotions or had had too much to drink. Probably both.

After letting out a long, hard breath, he said, "Murder?"

"It appears so," Miguel said soberly.

Officer Brummel slapped a hand over his mouth as

if to stifle a muscle jumping in his jaw and leaned back in his chair. "Who would've done this? And *why?*"

"That's what we intend to find out," Miguel said.

"Right. The reason I'm in this room, I'm the first to be questioned of the folks still waitin'." He stabbed his chest with his thumb. "I suppose I'm the prime suspect."

"I understand you're new to the Santa Bonita police department," Rosa said.

"That's right. Look—" he tilted his head toward Rosa but spoke to Miguel. "I get why you and Pike—" He nodded at the officer standing by the door. "—are doing this, but why your wife? And still in her weddin' dress, I might add."

"Rosa's a former constable with the London Metropolitan Police," Miguel said with pride in his voice. "She often consults with us."

"Oh?" Officer Brummel's eyes crinkled as if he found the information amusing. "You're the lady investigator I've heard about? I didn't make the connection."

"Like I said," Rosa began, "you're new."

"Right. I'm a temp, transferred in to cover for Nichols. Poor guy put his back out somethin' terrible.

Rosa lifted her chin and asked, "How did you meet Miss Winters?"

"Charlene was actin' in a show shot on Santa Monica's beach, and I was workin' security. Hollywood sometimes hires off-duty cops to work as security guards to keep the rubberneckers away. Especially when it's someone like Charlene. She tends, uh . . ." He cleared his throat. ". . . . *Tended* to attract a lot of gawkers. Anyway, we somehow got to talkin' on one of her breaks and . . . well, there you have it."

"Do you have family in LA?" Miguel asked.

"Naw. I'm originally from New York. Moved to California with my wife."

"Wife?" Rosa said with a cocked brow.

Officer Brummel blushed, then corrected. "Ex-wife. Sorry. Habit."

"How long have you been divorced?" Miguel asked.

"Uh, two years." Officer Brummel rubbed the back of his neck, then crossed his well-built arms. Rosa couldn't help but imagine how easy it would've been for him to bring that frying pan down on Charlene's head.

"She didn't like it out here," Officer Brummel continued. "Well, okay, there was probably more to it than that, but hey . . . I guess that's kind of off-topic, right? Anyway, yeah, two years. She's back in Jersey now. Much happier there, I'm sure."

Rosa noted how the man rambled about his ex-wife. Perhaps due to an excess of alcohol in his system or simply nerves.

"How would you describe the relationship between yourself and Miss Winters?" Rosa asked. The question was standard, but Rosa asked it to save Miguel any discomfort. "How well did the two of you get on?"

"We got on great. She's quite a firecracker or . . . she *was*, I mean."

"No arguments recently?" Miguel tapped the eraser end of a pencil on the desk.

"Look, Belmonte, I know what you're tryin' to do. But I don't got a motive here."

"You seemed pretty jealous," Rosa said.

Hank Brummel jerked his neck tightly to stare at her, but before he could object, Rosa said, "I saw you and Charlene standing by the fountain at my aunt's house. You looked as if you were having a lovers' quarrel."

"That was just a little misunderstanding. I'd only just found out that she and your husband shared a history."

"Were you upset that she hadn't told you sooner?" Rosa pressed.

"Sure! What guy wouldn't be? But like I said, I was just caught off guard. I wouldn't've killed her over it."

"Why did you leave the room?" Miguel asked.

Officer Brummel squinted. "What?"

"The estimated time of death given to us by Dr. Philpott was between six and six-thirty, which was when I sang to my lovely wife. The whole room was focused on the stage, but you chose that time to leave the room." Miguel's gaze had been on Rosa, but from the corner of his eye, he'd noticed Brummel leaving. Force of habit from years of police work. He added, "Why did you go?"

"Charlene found the music, well, upsettin'. Said she was goin' to the powder room. I decided I'd had enough, no offense. I left to call a cab."

"Did anyone see you?" Rosa asked. "In the foyer or outside?"

Officer Brummel lifted a shoulder. "Not that I know of."

"And what happened to the cab?" Rosa asked. "No one says they saw a cab waiting; no driver came in looking for his fare."

Scowling, Officer Brummel held up his hands. "I'm embarrassed, but these big mitts don't work so great on those dial wheels, especially if I've had a few. I also got the number wrong a few times; those numbers in the directory are pretty small. Anyway, just as I was about to dial the operator, I heard a commotion, and I came runnin' back into the reception hall."

Rosa shared a look with Miguel. They wouldn't be able to determine if Officer Brummel's story was true or not since he hadn't got through to anyone.

Miguel pushed away from the desk. "Okay, I think

we're done for now, Hank. I know I don't need to tell you this, but please don't leave town until further notice."

"Got no place to go," Officer Brummel said as he got to his feet. "And I'm still workin' at the precinct for at least a few weeks more."

"One last question before you go," Miguel started. "Do you know of anyone who might've had something against Charlene? Did she mention anything to you?"

Hank Brummel's eyebrows came together as he thought for a moment. "She did mention something about that Sussman guy?"

"Donald Sussman?" Rosa said. What could Aunt Louisa's friend have to do with Charlene?

"Yeah, him," Officer Brummel said. "She seemed shocked to see him here, at the wedding. I never met him personally."

"What did Charlene say about him?" Miguel asked.

"Nothing much." Officer Brummel shrugged. "I got the impression that she hadn't decided yet, but she did say she was tired of the guy harassin' her."

11

*R*osa immediately felt pity for Alicia Rodriguez, who looked like a frightened rabbit with her shoulders turned inward and her dark eyes wide and glassy.

"I went to the restroom," she said in her distinct Spanish accent. "It's the reason I left the hall. Something I ate, I think." Her reddened eyes darted between Rosa and Miguel. "I did not know I would miss such a special song."

"Was there anyone else in the restroom?" Rosa asked gently. She'd visited it in the past and knew there were six stalls and a counter with two sinks in the room.

Alicia lifted a thin shoulder. "I do not know. I cannot think. I am so worried I have upset Mr.

Forrester." She blinked back tears. "I do not want to lose my job."

"Miss Rodriguez, had you ever met Miss Winters in the past?" Miguel asked. "Maybe at another event?"

Alicia shook her head. "No, sir. I have never met her before. I never even seen her on the television. I am too busy working."

Rosa glanced at Miguel, hoping to relay her desire to let the poor girl go and relieve her of her anxiety.

With a slight nod, Miguel said. "That will be all for now, Miss Rodriguez."

Alicia clutched her purse. "I can go?"

"Yes," Rosa said. "Mr. Forrester is waiting in the foyer. He'll drive you home."

"*Gracias*. Thank you!" Alicia pushed out of her chair and practically fled out of the room.

Rosa stared as the nanny raced out. She was lithe, quick, and could've run from the kitchen to the reception hall in good time, but Rosa had a hard time imagining Alicia arranging a body in the bottom of a trolley. Clarence and Julie would've missed her in the time it would've taken.

She turned back to Miguel. "Who's left?"

"Miss Brinkley and Mr. Sussman."

"Right, my aunt's friend," Rosa said. "Shall we save him to the end?"

Miguel grinned, then playfully mimicked her English accent. "Yes, we shall."

Officer Pike brought Doris Brinkley into the room, and she took the empty chair. Rosa considered Miss Brinkley's disheveled look. Her bouffant had lost its perkiness—perhaps her hairspray hadn't been up to the task—and the cotton fabric of her dress was marred with horizontal wrinkle lines. She held a crumpled handkerchief to her face, sobbing intermittently into it. It seemed few were holding up well to the wedding party and its aftereffects.

"I just can't believe she's dead!" Miss Brinkley blew her nose, glancing up apologetically. "I'm sorry. It's just that she was so full of life, and, well, I've never seen a dead person before."

Rosa recalled seeing Miss Brinkley hovering when the body was discovered, her emotions opposite from the emotional display they witnessed now. However, shock sometimes caused a delay in emotional response.

"Where were you when the band was playing?" Rosa asked.

"The restroom. I was sick."

Rosa glanced at Miguel and asked, "Did you see anyone else there?" *Alicia Rodriguez, perhaps.*

"No. I was . . ." Miss Brinkley glanced sheepishly at Miguel, "indisposed. I wouldn't have noticed if anyone came in."

"But you returned to the reception hall," Rosa started, "in time to see Charlene's body."

"Yes, well, I felt better after—" Miss Brinkley motioned toward her throat, indicating she'd been vomiting. That would make two claiming illnesses from the food, a matter Rosa was certain Señora Morales would take issue with. However, if there had been a problem with the food, more people would surely complain about illness.

Rosa remembered seeing Miss Brinkley and Charlene speaking together, suggesting an animosity between them. "How were you and Miss Winters acquainted?" she asked.

"Oh." Miss Brinkley dabbed the corner of her eyes, which didn't help the black smudge of her mascara. "As I told you before, we're both actresses." Her eyes glazed over. "I want to be as famous as her."

Rosa lifted a brow and asked pointedly, "What were you and Miss Winters arguing about?"

Doris Brinkley hiccupped. "What?"

"I saw you and Miss Winters having words at the reception," Rosa said. "What were you arguing about?"

"Oh, that silly thing." Miss Brinkley giggled inappropriately, and Rosa wondered about the woman's state of mind. "I'd lent her my Bunchberry lipstick. She said it was hers and refused to give it back." Miss Brinkley cocked her head. "That's stealing."

Rosa glanced at Miguel.

"Miss Brinkley," Miguel started, "did you visit the staff restroom near the kitchen at any time today?"

"Excuse me?" Miss Brinkley's mouth dropped open. "Why on earth would I do that?"

"We have reason to believe that perhaps you did visit the restroom there," Rosa said. "It's more private."

"Is it?" Miss Brinkley blinked as if she was filing that information for later. "I didn't know that. And I don't know what you could mean by thinking I lied about which restroom I used." She huffed with indignation. "I think I would know that."

One would think that she would.

Miguel gave Rosa a questioning look, and Rosa shook her head to indicate she had nothing more to ask. Miss Brinkley smoothed out her skirt and patted her hair before exiting the room like a model on a catwalk.

12

*D*onald Sussman stared at Miguel and Rosa with impatience across his face as he sat in Father Navarro's office. Rosa stared back with curiosity. Her aunt's friend wore the same black business suit he had worn the night before at the rehearsal party at the Forrester mansion, the tie now loose and his suit jacket wrinkled. Rosa wondered about his health. His face was flush, and his breath heavy—as if he had just climbed a long flight of stairs.

He narrowed his gaze on Miguel. "Left me 'til last, huh?"

"Someone has to be last," Miguel said.

"These Mexican weddings go too long." Mr. Sussman made a point of looking at his watch.

Miguel cocked his head. "Are you in a hurry?"

Mr. Sussman huffed. "I'd love to hurry right out of here."

"You've had experience with long wedding traditions, haven't you?" Rosa asked. "Didn't Aunt Louisa mention that your son married a Latina lady?"

Ducking his chin, Mr. Sussman regarded Rosa suspiciously. "That's right."

"Did they get married in Santa Bonita?" Miguel asked.

"Buenos Aires."

"Your daughter-in-law is Argentinian, then?" Miguel said.

The man sighed. "Yes. What of it? Can we just please get on with this?"

Rosa recalled the phone call that had taken Mr. Sussman away from the party at the Forresters. She made a mental note to question her aunt further about what she knew about this man who was perpetually in a hurry.

"What do you do for a living, Mr. Sussman?" Miguel asked.

Mr. Sussman folded his arms over his chest. "That's got nothing to do with this, has it?"

"It might," Rosa said. "The job of the police is to get all the background information available on anyone who might be, or might eventually be on the suspect list."

"Suspect list!"

"It's only a formality, Mr. Sussman," Rosa said calmly. "Proper police procedure to interview those in the crime's vicinity who can't clearly show where they were at the time. You understand, I'm sure."

"With all due respect Mrs. Belmonte . . ." Mr. Sussman paused as he looked at Rosa. "Ah, I was just wondering why on earth you are involved with this interview, but I remember now your aunt said you're a lady investigator."

"She often consults with the Santa Bonita Police Department," Miguel said. "Now, can you please answer the question? What do you do for a living?"

"All right. I'm retired." Mr. Sussman pulled at his tie and continued. "I was in live theater production for many years in San Francisco and Los Angeles. Not as an actor or producer, mind you, but I invested in several shows that did well over time. Before that, I was in real estate and did fine in that field too."

"But now you're involved with an advisory board here in Santa Bonita," Rosa said, recalling what her aunt had mentioned.

"That's right. I've served on other arts councils in the past, so I have an interest in anything to do with that. I like it here in Santa Bonita. I think there is great potential for more filmmaking."

"How well did you know Charlene Winters?" Miguel asked.

"Not that well, but we did run into each other occasionally in the course of her work."

"So, you had no relationship with her outside of that?" Miguel pressed.

"As I said, not really, no." Donald Sussman leaned back in his chair and casually crossed his legs, trying to give the impression that he was relaxed and not in a hurry. Rosa wasn't sure, but she got a distinct feeling it might be a physical reaction, unconscious or not, to a line of questioning that made him uncomfortable. She had seen it before in people who were practiced at lying. Their bodily reactions were primed to convey the exact opposite of their feelings.

"Are you involved in any organizations other than at City Hall?" Rosa asked.

"Well, I dabble in a few things." Mr. Sussman pulled out a package of cigarettes from the side pocket of his suit jacket. "Do you mind?" He waved the package in the air.

"No, go ahead," Miguel said.

Mr. Sussman languidly tapped out a cigarette, put the package back in his pocket, and lit up.

"Such as?" Rosa asked, noting that she suddenly now had to tease information out of him.

"Such as?" the man returned.

Rosa repeated, "Are you involved in any other organizations?"

After a long plume of smoke, he said, "I help sponsor and run workshops and such."

"Workshops?" Miguel said. "For whom?"

"Aspiring actors, playwrights, directors," Mr. Sussman replied. "People like that. We try to elevate the art form by enriching them with better skills and such."

"That's interesting," Rosa said. "Was Miss Winters involved in any way?"

Mr. Sussman tapped the ash of his cigarette into an ashtray on the desk. "As I said, I didn't know her that well."

"Who runs the workshops?"

After a long pull on his cigarette, Mr. Sussman said, "A group called the New National Theater Coalition."

"And you're part of that coalition?" Miguel asked.

"Yes," Mr. Sussman returned coyly. "On a casual basis, of course."

"Based in Santa Bonita?" Rosa asked.

"No, Los Angeles."

Rosa returned, "Organizations like that would benefit greatly from someone like Charlene Winters endorsing or being part of them, wouldn't you say?"

Mr. Sussman's eyebrows came together as he waved his cigarette. "I'm not sure what you mean?"

"Did you ever think about asking her to talk about such an organization publicly?" Miguel asked.

Mr. Sussman shrugged. "I may have mentioned it to her."

Miguel leaned in. "And what was her reaction?"

"As I recall, she said she would think about it. Anyway, that's as far as that ever went." Mr. Sussman uncrossed his legs, his look of restlessness returning. "Strange line of questioning, isn't it? I mean, what on earth has all that got to do with anything."

"Where did you go while Detective Belmonte was onstage?" Rosa asked. "Several people saw you leaving the room."

Donald Sussman lifted the cigarette to his mouth but stopped midair to look at it. "Sometimes a man wants to enjoy a cigarette away from the din of a noisy room." He grinned at Miguel. "Nothing against your singing, by the way. I just wanted some fresh air."

"Did anyone see you loitering about outside?" Miguel asked.

"I never noticed." Mr. Sussman stubbed out his cigarette, its final plumes stretching to the ceiling. "That's what this is all about, huh? The murder happened during the singing?"

Miguel nodded. "We were all there, of course, but the pathologist has confirmed it."

"Do you know of anyone, perhaps someone in the entertainment world, who might have had something against Miss Winters?" Rosa asked. "Particularly anyone who might've been there today?"

Donald Sussman shook his head slowly.

Miguel held the man's gaze. "Can you think of anyone with ill will toward her in any sense?"

"Well, let me think." He eyed the dead cigarette in the ashtray as if he regretted stubbing it out so soon. "There's Miss Brinkley."

Rosa tucked a stray brunette curl behind her ear. "Doris Brinkley, the actress?"

"*Aspiring* actress," Mr. Sussman clarified. "She is a bit of an odd bird. I don't know if she had any real animosity toward Miss Winters, but she spoke disparagingly of her to me once."

"How so?" Rosa asked.

"Just criticizing her acting skills, mostly. She said that Charlene didn't really know how to make the character believable and the usual stuff you would hear from a rival actress. The thing is, not ten minutes later, I overheard her praising Miss Winters' acting skills to her face at the same party. That struck me as very disingenuous, to say the least."

"What do you mean by saying she is an odd bird?" Rosa asked.

"For one thing, she doesn't seem to have a lot of friends, and there are rumors that she has a temper and is easily offended. And someone writes scathing reviews in the entertainment magazines and newspapers anonymously about Charlene's acting." Donald Sussman gave Rosa a pointed look. "I've heard it said that Doris Brinkley is behind those. Jealousy makes people do crazy things."

13

Rosa couldn't be happier than how she felt the next morning when she woke up beside Miguel in his house. Her home now, *finally*. Like many homes in Santa Bonita, the small dwelling was a white-stucco abode with red-tile ceilings and had a yard dotted with palms and trees producing citrus fruit. Inside were the standard terra-cotta floor tiles, which Miguel had adorned with Turkish-style floor rugs, and on the walls were Mediterranean paintings with plenty of ocean blues.

The long wait to be open about living together as a married couple was over. No more sneaking around like guilty teenagers or getting snitched on by one loud and mischievous African gray parrot named Homer.

The bird liked to hang around the kitchen during mealtimes, and Rosa had already threatened to put him back in his cage if he dared to land on the table. She'd figured that if he didn't watch it, she might just return him to the precinct. He was supposed to go there while Rosa and Miguel were scheduled to be away on a second honeymoon, but Rosa wasn't beyond sending him there for a stay, anyway.

"Homer, good birdy. Homer, good bird."

Rosa took a bite of her toast, choosing to ignore the parrot. No sense in reinforcing bad behavior. Miguel, apparently, had other ideas on how to appease Homer and stealthily ripped off small pieces of the crust and tossed them to the bird.

"You're training him to beg," Rosa said.

"At least I'm training him," Miguel returned with a grin. Rosa smiled at her handsome husband, his hair messed and his jaw darkening with bristles. She liked the rough and tumble look, but not as much as when he was clean-shaven and his hair, short at the temples and longer on top, was oiled and swept to the side.

"No mass today?" Rosa asked over the rim of her coffee cup.

Miguel's look was an unasked question. Did Rosa want to go to mass? Not particularly, especially when they were supposed to be on a second honeymoon. They had a lot to do, even if most of the town was closed.

Rosa ran fingers through her short, dark waves. Her

skin was freshly scrubbed and makeup-free except for a layer of peach-colored lipstick. She was a newlywed, after all, and wanted to look nice for her husband. "Let's take a week off. We need to pick up Diego soon. Now that we're not going on honeymoon, I'm sure Aunt Louisa would appreciate it." Aunt Louisa was the only one at the mansion who hadn't bonded with Rosa's adopted feline, but her aunt was the head of the household, and what she thought and felt was paramount, always.

Thinking of her aunt made her think about poor Elliot Roundtree. The ranch manager was obviously smitten with Aunt Louisa, but he was fighting an uphill battle. Even if Aunt Louisa had feelings for the rugged outdoorsman, and Rosa believed she did, her long-ingrained sense of propriety and a person's proper place in society would stop her from acting on it. How others perceived her was more important to Aunt Louisa than what her own heart desired.

Rosa's gaze returned to Miguel, who was staring at her.

"You're so beautiful, Mrs. Belmonte."

Rosa felt her smile stretch across her face, and if it weren't for this dratted murder case, she'd drag her husband back to the bedroom.

"Thank you, Mr. Belmonte. Now finish your breakfast. We've got a lot of work to do."

Miguel opened his mouth as if to protest, then his shoulders dropped. "You're right, of course, my dear, but when this is over—" Miguel pulled Rosa to her feet and kissed her passionately.

Homer squawked, "That's amore!"

Rosa broke out laughing. "That's the worst rendition of Dean Martin I've ever heard!"

Miguel grinned. "That's what I get for leaving the radio on to keep him company."

They nearly did the tango as they shuffled around each other to get dressed, and Rosa couldn't help but think of her room back at the Forrester mansion, which was twice the size with a much larger bed and a built-in closet. It was more spacious, but Rosa didn't have a problem being in close quarters with Miguel.

"Have you heard from the precinct?" Rosa asked as she chose a dress from their *shared* closet. Crime didn't take Sundays off, and neither did the police department.

"The guys are doing background checks on everyone without a solid alibi." Miguel tucked his shirt into his khaki pants. "After we get your cat, I'll call in to see if anything interesting has popped up."

Rosa selected a silk headscarf with a floral print which she tied neatly under her chin. She added a pair of short white gloves and her red-framed cat-eye sunglasses, then headed out the front door with Miguel.

Homer squawked after them, "Bye, bye, love!"

Santa Bonita was a seaside town that smelled of saline air from the Pacific Ocean. Much of the town was built in the south-European style, with white-stucco exteriors and prominent red-tile rooftops. Unlike Europe, the boulevards were wide, and more people drove than walked, but with so much distance to cover without the aid of trains, automobiles felt necessary here. What was once considered frivolous and ostentatious in the war years had become commonplace as the post-war boom gave families more income than they had ever enjoyed before, and the number of cars on the road was a testament to that.

The Forrester mansion was on a sprawling estate found on the north end of town. The road led up a hill with outstanding vistas of the Pacific Ocean. The long driveway from the road to the mansion was lined with tall palms.

With one hand on the steering wheel of his blue 1954 Plymouth Plaza sedan, Miguel gave Rosa a quick look. Reaching over to squeeze her arm, he said, "I can't believe you gave all this up to be with me."

"Well, it's not really mine to give up," Rosa said. "It's not like I owned it." She grinned wryly. "Aunt

Louisa has assured me my bedroom will be there for me, should I ever need it in the future."

Miguel snorted. "And here I thought I'd finally won her over."

They reached the front of the mansion, slowing around the three-tier concrete fountain and stopping near the front door. They weren't planning on staying long, otherwise, Miguel would've parked closer to the six-car garage.

Rosa noted how Miguel hung back a step or two as they approached the massive wooden doors of the vast Mediterranean-style house with its terra-cotta-color stucco exterior and red-tile roof.

"Now that I've officially moved out, I suppose I should ring the bell," Rosa said as she pressed the button.

Instead of one of the maids, Rosa was surprised to find Clarence standing behind the opened door. "Why are you ringing the bell?" he said without a proper greeting.

Rosa answered in kind. "Why are you answering the door?"

Miguel scratched his chin. "Why wouldn't he answer the door?"

"I'm taking Julie out for ice cream; then we're picking Alicia up from her baseball game. She plays in a ladies' league. After yesterday's ordeal, I gave her the night off."

"Yes, well, I suppose she needed the break," Rosa said, stepping inside. "We're just here to pick up Diego."

"Check with Señora Gomez. I think he's in the kitchen."

Rosa smiled, thinking about her gray-brown tabby curled up on the red-tile floor in the kitchen under a beam of sunlight, and sure enough, that was exactly where she found him.

"Diego!" Rosa scooped him into her arms and buried her chin in his neck. "Have you been a good boy?"

"*Muy bueno*," Señora Gomez said. "*No problemo.* We will miss the little *gato* when he's gone."

"We'll visit a lot," Rosa said. "I promise. Now, I believe I left a satchel here to carry him."

"*Sí.* I'll find it for you, Miss Rosa." The housekeeper's eyes widened. "Forgive me. I mean, *Mrs.* Belmonte."

Rosa laughed. "You can continue to call me Miss Rosa." Though Rosa loved being Miguel's wife, the title of Mrs. Belmonte still made her think of Miguel's mother.

"I thought I heard guests." Rosa and Miguel turned to the sound of Aunt Louisa's voice.

Aunt Louisa was dressed impeccably in a fine-knit, short-sleeved sweater, a pencil skirt, and a wide belt. Her two-inch pumps clicked on the floor tiles as she crossed the room.

"Good morning, Aunt Louisa," Rosa said. "We've just dropped in to pick up Diego."

Aunt Louisa cast a disapproving glance Miguel's way. "I thought you were going on a honeymoon to Victoria?"

"Yes, well, since the unfortunate death last night . . ." Rosa began.

Miguel jumped in. "We both thought we'd have a nicer time away if we solved this case first."

Aunt Louisa harrumphed, then turned her attention to Señora Gomez. "I'll take a coffee out on the patio."

"Yes, ma'am," Señora Gomez said promptly. "I'll make a fresh pot."

Aunt Louisa politely asked, "Would you like to join me?"

Miguel cast a nervous look, and Rosa said, "Unfortunately, we have a busy morning booked and must leave shortly. But thank you for the offer." Changing the subject, Rosa asked, "Is Gloria at home? Don't tell me she's still asleep?"

Aunt Louisa sat around the kitchen table as she waited for her coffee to percolate. "As you know,

Gloria can sleep until noon, but no. She's gone for breakfast with Jake Wilson."

The way she said "Jake Wilson," Rosa gathered that her aunt hadn't accepted him as a possible son-in-law. As a journalist, he was a step up from Gloria's other dates, who were actors or college students, but Rosa knew her aunt was hoping for a doctor or lawyer.

Until Rosa had gone to London and come back married to Miguel, Aunt Louisa had continued to mourn the "one that had gotten away" for Rosa. Dr. Larry Rayburn was once the assistant medical examiner in Santa Bonita. Rosa liked Larry but hadn't gotten over Miguel enough to fall in love. Besides, Larry had moved to Texas, and Rosa had already established Rosa Reed Investigations in Santa Bonita.

Darla, one of Aunt Louisa's many maids, stepped into the kitchen. "Ma'am, the telephone rang, and a gentleman is on the line. Mr. Roundtree, ma'am."

Aunt Louisa quickly moved to stand, but when her eyes grazed over Rosa and Miguel, she relaxed back into her chair. "Please let Mr. Roundtree know I'm indisposed."

"Don't delay your conversation on our account," Rosa said.

Aunt Louisa shot Rosa a dark look. "I'm certainly not doing that. I'm not about to jump at every Tom,

Dick, or Harry that decides to call the house. I'll call him back when it's convenient."

Rosa stared at her aunt. Her response was stronger than what was called for in the circumstances. Besides, Rosa *knew* Elliot Roundtree wasn't just another Tom, Dick, or Harry. She'd seen the two in an intimate embrace when they hadn't known they were being watched.

Miguel broke the awkward silence. "If the telephone isn't being used, would you mind if I made a quick call? I need to check in with my officers at the precinct."

"Of course." Aunt Louisa waved her fingers as if dismissing him. "Rosa can show you where to find it."

Rosa was thankful for the ruse to leave her bristly aunt. The coffee was ready, so her aunt stepped outside, Señora Gomez following with a cup of coffee on a tray. Rosa placed her sleepy cat into the satchel and led Miguel out of the kitchen.

Miguel spoke under his breath. "Your aunt makes my mother look like a saint."

"She's just upset that I've taken what I want while she refuses to."

Miguel raised a brow. "You mean a fellow from the wrong side of the tracks?"

Rosa linked her arm with his and smiled. "Precisely." She led Miguel down the hallway to Aunt Louisa's office. The room was larger than Rosa's new living room in the house she shared with Miguel. It had a large wooden desk, a large floor rug, and a sofa for a visitor or for one to catch a quick nap. Rosa had a sudden urge to do just that but remained standing to avoid the risk of nodding off.

Miguel immediately went to the telephone and dialed. After getting Officer Pike on the line, he continued to make humming noises, his brow wrinkling in a way that Rosa thought endearing.

"Is that so?" he said with a whistle. "In that case, I think I'd like to talk to him again."

Rosa held Miguel's gaze as he hung up the telephone. "What is it, darling?"

Miguel pinched his lips. "It seems Officer Hank Brummel is still very much married."

14

*R*osa breathed deeply with relief as she stepped out of the Forrester mansion with Miguel on one arm and the satchel holding Diego on the other. She appreciated all the time she'd lived under her aunt's roof and all the care and support she and Grandma Sally had given. Even so, it was immensely satisfying to finally be on her own, a married woman, and independent in her own right.

Placing Diego in the middle of the bench seat, Rosa slipped inside Miguel's Plymouth. Her own gorgeous pearly white Corvette with its luscious red-leather interior remained tucked away in the large garage of the Forrester mansion. Rosa didn't want to admit it to Miguel, but she didn't feel it fit in the neighborhood where she now lived with him. Perhaps one day, she'd trade it in for something a little less ostentatious, but the thought of giving it up made her stomach twist a little.

Rosa glanced at the sleeping fluff ball. He and Miguel's parrot were acquainted, but they hadn't spent any time together recently, and Rosa didn't want to leave them unattended. "I don't think we should subject him to Homer's singing just yet, not to mention his sharp beak."

Miguel grinned. "Good call."

"Why don't we visit Dr. Philpott," Rosa suggested. "Perhaps he has new information for us."

Miguel's smile fell, and Rosa immediately felt terrible about bringing up Charlene's death and the image of her body on a slab, which had ignited the idea. She added quickly, "Or we could just phone him."

Miguel started the engine and steered his car around the fountain and down the long drive. "No, we can drop in at the morgue," he said. "It's on the way."

Rosa put her sunglasses on and delighted in the sunlight glistening off the ocean and the waves crashing large and white against the shore. She reached over Diego's head to lay a hand on Miguel's shoulder. How many wives could suggest an outing to the local morgue and their husbands think it a good idea? Rosa smiled to herself, feeling very fortunate.

The morgue in Santa Bonita was at the back of the

small hospital, which to Rosa, at first glance, looked more like a boutique hotel. Only one story, the hospital was painted white to fight against the sun's heat. Clusters of palm trees and neatly mowed lawns surrounded the property, which was nothing like the three- or four-story brick-and-stone hospitals in London.

Inside, Rosa followed Miguel, who'd insisted on carrying Diego, down a wide hallway and through the door leading to the morgue's office area. It wasn't the first time Diego had accompanied Rosa, and the on-duty nurse didn't seem surprised to see the cat. Instead, she put on a voice reserved for small children and patted Diego on his head.

"Diego! So nice to see you again."

"Is Dr. Philpott on the premises?" Rosa asked.

The nurse nodded toward the hallway. "He's in the morgue. Just finished an autopsy. I don't think he'll mind if you go in."

Miguel handed Diego to Rosa before opening the door to the morgue. Immediately Rosa's senses were assaulted with the stringent smell of bleach and embalming solution. It was enough to make Diego's nose twitch, but not enough to wake him.

Rosa had prepared herself to view the body of Charlene Winters, which lay on the surgical table in the center of the room, a sheet pulled up discreetly to her neck. Her skin, marble-like in its paleness, could only exist on someone who'd taken their last breath. Charlene's face had been cleaned of makeup, her hair combed off her face. Even in death, she had Hollywood beauty.

"Howdy," Dr. Philpott said. "I wondered if I'd see the two of you today." His eyes landed on Diego, who poked his head out of the satchel with narrow, sleepy eyes. "Or should I say, the three of you?"

Miguel, who looked rather pale as he stared at Charlene's corpse, got straight to business. "Do you have anything of note to report? Were there any defensive wounds?"

Dr. Philpott paused before answering. "No defensive wounds," he said. "Her fingernails were clean, and no scratching or bruising on her arms. The only injury is the deep indentation on her skull. Rather, two."

"Two injuries?" Rosa asked.

"I didn't notice the second one at first," Dr. Philpott said, "as it was slighter that the other, and hidden by the blood."

"I see," Rosa said, and sensing there was more, added, "and?"

"We ran the normal tests," Dr. Philpott began. He untied his apron and threw it into a dirty laundry container. Then he turned to face them. "Miss Winters was expecting."

Miguel's jaw dropped. "Pregnant?"

Rosa glanced at the flat stomach of the body. Dr. Philpott answered her unspoken question. "She was about twelve weeks."

Rosa locked her gaze on Miguel's brown eyes. "That would be motive for Officer Brummel."

15

The next day, Officer Hank Brummel, on duty and in full uniform, sat in Miguel's office trying to win over the affections of Diego, who was sprawled out on the floor, observing.

"I've always had a way with cats," Officer Brummel said as he reached to stroke Diego's head with his huge hand.

Diego's ears went flat, his eyes narrowed, and he ducked his head slightly under the officer's touch while his tail swished slowly back and forth.

"I've seen him take a man's arm off," Miguel said with a barely hidden smirk as he watched Diego's reaction.

Hank Brummel chortled but withdrew his hand.

"That was a while ago," Miguel continued mildly, "but once they've tasted human blood..."

"Detective Belmonte!" Rosa scolded.

"Sorry, just kidding. He's really a sweetheart."

"Yes, he is," Rosa agreed.

"That incident with the neighbor's French poodle was just a misunderstanding," Miguel said nonchalantly as he took out his notepad from his top drawer. "We made sure Fifi had a nice funeral. I'm sure Mrs. Gonzales will find another dog soon."

Rosa rolled her eyes. Miguel sometimes liked to needle suspects who he suspected had lied to him.

"Okay, I get it," Officer Brummel said uneasily. "You're kiddin' me." He glanced down at Diego, who stared at him balefully.

Folding his arms, Officer Brummel asked, "What did you want to see me about?"

Miguel's expression grew serious as he leaned forward, propped his elbows on his desk, and clasped his hands in front of him. He looked at Hank Brummel for a long moment before sighing. "I don't know what it's like in Los Angeles, but here at the Santa Bonita precinct, we don't often have officers lie during a murder investigation."

Hank Brummel blinked rapidly, and his face lost some of its color. "Whatcha mean?"

"You're married, aren't you?" Rosa said.

"To a . . ." Miguel consulted his notes. ". . . Marjorie Brummel, formerly Marjorie Greening. You told us you were divorced and that your former wife lived in New Jersey."

"I . . ."

"Did you think we wouldn't check you out?" Miguel asked. "This was information our department found out with just a couple of phone calls."

There was silence in the room for a few minutes as Officer Hank Brummel leaned forward and hid his face in his hands.

Rosa cleared her throat, then asked, "Does Mrs. Brummel know about Charlene Winters?"

Officer Brummel shook his head. "Look, I know guys say this all the time, but I've never done anything like this. It just kind of happened. Charlene mesmerized me. I lost my head." He looked at the ceiling for a moment as if confessing to God. "I love my wife; I really do. It just . . . happened. I have no excuse."

"I'm sure you're aware of how this looks?" Miguel said.

"I know, I know," Officer Brummel blurted. "But I didn't kill her! I barely even knew her. I didn't love her or anything. It was just . . . I don't know what it was. But I didn't kill her. Why would I?"

"Perhaps she was going to tell your wife?" Rosa said.

"No, she would never have done that. It was just a fling! We weren't serious; we both knew it wouldn't last. She was the one who kept saying she didn't want strings attached, and I agreed."

"No strings attached, huh?" Miguel said.

"Exactly," Officer Brummel said.

Rosa grimaced. As if that got him off the hook for cheating on his wife. "I would think a baby constitutes attached strings, wouldn't you?"

Officer Brummel's head jerked back. "*What?*"

"Because this is very obviously a murder case," Miguel began, "the pathologist decided to check a bit further on a hunch. Charlene was twelve weeks pregnant. By my calculations, you two started dating around twelve weeks ago. Isn't that right?"

Clearly at a loss for words, Hank Brummel gaped.

Miguel rubbed his chin, his eyes on Rosa. "Here's what I think, Rosa. Maybe it's at the wedding, between the wedding and the reception, or just before the wedding, in the car, but Charlene decides to tell Hank about her condition at some point. That's bad for Hank; really, really bad. Naturally, he panics about it. His marriage, the one he lied to us about, will probably end badly. He is going to be humiliated. The woman he admits he doesn't even love will need him to support her and her child for a very long time. Hank doesn't know what to do. Then, as she gets up to use a restroom, he gets an idea. If Charlene is gone, so are all of his problems."

"Sounds plausible, so far," Rosa nodded.

"No, that's not what happened at all!" Hank shouted.

Diego, startling awake from a dead sleep, glared at him with disdain.

Regaining his composure, he said, "I went to call a cab."

"You told us you had had too much to drink to drive, and Charlene didn't like to drive," Miguel said.

"That's right. That's why I called a cab."

"Unfortunately, no one saw you go outside."

"And then there's the problem of the bartender," Rosa added.

Officer Brummel narrowed his eyes. "What problem?"

"According to the officer who interviewed him, he said he only served you one drink," Miguel said. "A single bottle of Corona beer. Hardly enough to get drunk on. Especially for a guy your size."

Officer Brummel leaned back, and his arms tightened around his chest. "I get why I would be your prime suspect, but you're barking up the wrong tree." His jaw twitched. "I think I'd like to call my lawyer now."

. . .

THE OFFICES of *The Santa Bonita Morning Star* on a Monday were as frantic as Rosa would have imagined a much larger newspaper in New York or London might be. The bullpen was shared by secretaries and journalists, who all seemed to attack typewriters, answer ringing phones, and converse in loud volumes.

"I wouldn't have thought there was this much news going on in our little *pueblo*," Miguel commented as he observed several people hurrying down the long hallway that led to the main bullpen area.

"I suppose it's inevitable that Santa Bonita will keep growing," Rosa said as she grabbed Miguel's arm to pull him out of the way of a young woman pushing a trolley full of file folders as she came careening out of an office.

"Excuse me," the young woman said without looking back as she continued down the hall toward two offices with frosted-glass partitions—perhaps occupied by the upper management of the editorial staff.

"Hiya!" Gloria said when she spotted them. "Are you looking for me?"

"Actually, we were hoping to talk to Jake," Rosa said.

"Oh." Gloria flashed a brief look of disappointment. "He has his own office now, just down the hall. He says it comes with the promise of promotion soon."

"How wonderful," Rosa added.

Gloria raised a brow. "So, what's buzzin', cousin?"

"Sorry?" Rosa was still catching on to all the youth slang. She shot an inquisitive look at Miguel, who grinned in return.

"Rosa." Gloria placed dainty hands on her hips. "You promised me leads before anybody else got them."

After Miguel lifted a shoulder, Rosa turned to her cousin. "Very well. What can you tell us about Doris Brinkley?"

"Doris?" Gloria's eyes widened at the question. "Not much. We hung out a bit on set when I was acting. We know each other, but I wouldn't say we're friends."

"Donald Sussman referred to her as an 'odd bird,'" Rosa said. "Would you categorize her that way, too?"

Gloria sniffed. "I can imagine Mr. Sussman saying something like that. Talk about an odd bird!" Gloria sat on the edge of her desk. "But yeah, Doris is . . . different."

"In what way?" Miguel asked.

"She's, I don't know, really intense? For example, she'll get excited about something that another person might think is no big deal or go ape about, something that should be considered only an irritation."

"Did you ever hear her talk about Charlene Winters?" Rosa asked.

"Sure. Who didn't talk about Charlene Winters? But again, with Doris, she thought Charlene was the cat's meow one minute, and then she would tear her down the next."

"Can you give an example?" Miguel asked.

Gloria worked her lips. "Well, behind Miss Winters' back, Doris would say she dressed like a hussy and that she was a second-rate actress. But when Charlene Winters was in the room, she would act starstruck. I think she was obsessed with Miss Winters."

"Is there anything else you can think of?" Rosa asked.

"Actually," Gloria started, "I happened to be talking to our entertainment editor, Fred Worthington, about Miss Winters' death. He mentioned that Miss Winters had been disparaged in the fan reviews section."

"Fan reviews section?" Miguel asked.

"It's a section in *The Morning Star* where anyone from Santa Bonita can submit a review of a movie or a play. Mr. Worthington said there was one contributor who consistently wrote bad reviews about Miss Winters."

"I would like to read those reviews," Rosa said.

Gloria removed the pencil from behind her ear. "As it so happens, I did a little digging already on my own." She plopped a couple of newspapers on her desk and flipped them open. "Have a look. They're signed 'Anonymous,' so I don't know how they'll help."

Rosa took a few minutes to peruse the reviews, which were indeed, unflattering, then handed the newspapers to Miguel. She turned back to Gloria. "By the way, do you think you could use your skills as an investigative journalist to look into Donald Sussman for us?"

"What do you want to know?" Gloria asked.

"Anything that pops out that seems odd or of interest. He supports an organization called the New National Theater Commission."

Gloria scribbled the name down on a sheet of paper and nodded. "If I find out anything, I'll let you know."

Miguel gave the newspapers back to Gloria. "Thanks for this."

Gloria smiled brightly, like one who clearly enjoyed her job. "You're welcome, Detective."

16

Diego was still fast asleep in his satchel on the front seat of the two-door Plymouth, parked in the shade of an oak tree. A breeze swept in from the ocean, and with the windows cracked, the interior was comfortably cool. Rosa's pet gave her the briefest narrow-eyed look before returning to whatever blissful dream he'd been having.

"Shall we find Miss Brinkley?" Rosa asked.

"Way ahead of you." Miguel pulled his car onto the roadway and headed south. A crooked grin appeared. "I called the Blaze Talent Agency offices, the Los Angeles-based firm that handles Doris Brinkley and a stable of other actors and actresses. Apparently, Miss Brinkley can be found shooting a new commercial at Maverick Studios today."

"In Santa Bonita?"

"Yeah. Movie and TV studios seem to be popping up every day. We're close to Los Angeles without the big-city hullabaloo."

"I wonder if we'll start seeing more celebrities around town."

Miguel nodded. "Just last week, I saw Debbie Reynolds down at Bernie's Fried Chicken," Miguel said.

"You did not!" Rosa slapped his leg.

"Ow. Okay, maybe it wasn't her. Maybe her stunt double or something. But I did see Kirk Douglas coming out of that big mansion near your aunt's place that sold last month," Miguel said, keeping his eyes straight ahead.

"A glimpse of Kirk Douglas would certainly be exciting," she said brightly, then she was suddenly suspicious. She eyed her husband through her cat-eye sunglasses. "Are you sure? How do you know it was him?"

"Well, for one thing, he still had on that cowboy hat. The holster too. You remember the one from that movie we saw last month at the theater, *Gunfight at the O.K. Corral?*"

Rosa nudged his arm. "You know, I can tell when you're pulling my leg."

Miguel laughed. "Okay. That was probably a stunt double, too."

"Your mother might be right, you know," Rosa said.

Miguel gave her a sideways glance. "About what?"

"Perhaps Mario *is* funnier."

"Ouch!"

"But don't worry, you'll manage to get by on good looks alone," Rosa teased.

Miguel brought the car to a stop in front of a medium-sized single-story warehouse building that looked like it had been freshly erected.

Maverick Studios was a new television production facility built on an acre lot just south of town. Apparently, Donald Sussman was correct. Santa Bonita was fast becoming a favored shooting location for not only movies but apparently for television as well.

The studio didn't look all that large on the outside, smaller than a department store. Still, after Miguel had shown his detective badge to a burly security guard and they could walk through the front office section, the place suddenly seemed massive.

Rosa spotted Doris Brinkley standing at the far end of the dark, massive room in front of one of those huge RCA cameras with the rotating lenses. A small group of men stood behind the camera, including what must have been the cameraman and a director. Doris Brinkley and an attractive red-haired woman of about the same age stood in a set that looked like someone's backyard. The backdrop was painted and lit to look like a summer day, and was striking against the darkly lit ambiance of the rest of the great room.

The women were dressed in bland cotton A-line dresses in small floral print, with waists cinched uncomfortably tight. Men's handkerchiefs, tied at the nape of the neck, covered their short hair. They stood between two clotheslines with white linens and children's clothes hanging from them.

Rosa and Miguel tried to walk quietly on the smooth pavement floor so as not to disturb the shooting.

"I wish I could get my clothes as white as yours!" The red-haired woman said as she pointed to the clothesline directly behind Doris Brinkley.

"You can, Marg," Doris Brinkley said enthusiastically as she held up a large brightly colored detergent box. "It's easy! I use FAB soap for all my washing. It whitens better than any other soap in the world and does it without bleach! My husband's shirts come out much whiter, even in hard water!"

"Cut!" a man with a clipboard shouted. "Good job, ladies. We'll return after lunch for a couple more takes, but I think we got most of it."

When Rosa saw that Doris Brinkley had noticed her and Miguel standing off to one side, she gave a little wave. Looking perplexed, Miss Brinkley placed the detergent box on a table and strode toward them.

Cocking her head, she quipped, "I'm surprised to see you newlyweds here."

"Sorry to interrupt," Miguel said. "Your agency told us we'd find you here."

Looking doe-eyed, Miss Brinkley muttered, "Oh, okay."

"Is there somewhere we can talk in private?" Rosa asked.

A few minutes later, they sat in another set at the other end of the central area. This one had been set up to look like the interior of a doctor's office. There was a reception desk, a door with a sign labeled Dr. Schumann, and several upholstered chairs. There was even a small coffee table with a scattering of magazines and an ashtray. As soon as they were seated, Doris Brinkley pulled out a package of cigarettes and lit one up.

"Do you like shooting commercials?" Rosa asked.

"It pays the bills." The end of Miss Brinkley's cigarette lit up red as she inhaled. While exhaling a plume of smoke, she asked, "So what's this about?"

"We just want to ask you a few more questions," Miguel said.

"I gathered that," Miss Brinkley returned snidely. "But I can't imagine what more I can say. It's terrible what happened to Charlene. I didn't see anything, and when the murder happened, I was having a rough time in the bathroom."

"We're trying to ascertain motive from anyone who might know her," Miguel explained. "Did she ever talk to you about her relationship with Hank Brummel?"

Doris Brinkley snorted derisively and looked down for a long moment at her cigarette.

"Miss Brinkley?" Rosa prodded.

The actress replied triumphantly, "Charlene wanted Officer Brummel to marry her."

"How do you know that?" Rosa asked.

Miss Brinkley stared at Rosa with a strange, almost conspiratorial look. "She told me."

"Do you find that surprising?" Rosa asked. "I understand they had only been dating for a few months."

Miss Brinkley shrugged. "I can't explain it either. I think she could have done so much better than that muscle head. He didn't want to get married so soon because I guess he was recently divorced."

"What did you think of Charlene's acting skills?" Miguel asked.

Miss Brinkley frowned. "What's that got to do with anything?"

"Normal procedure, Miss Brinkley," Miguel said, "We are just trying to get—"

"Charlene was mediocre at best," Doris Brinkley said.

"Is that so?" Rosa said. "She was very popular."

"She had sex appeal, Mrs. Belmonte. That doesn't mean she could act. That blinded the directors who chose her." A sneer spread across her face. "I mean, did you see her in *Hearts and Wheels*?" Doris Brinkley laughed out loud while tapping her cigarette in the ashtray. "Whoever cast her for that role made a huge mistake."

"Do you think you would have done better in that role?" Rosa asked.

"Pfft. I know I would have," Miss Brinkley said quickly. "Charlene had serviceable acting skills, but she never could rise to a serious role."

Rosa got the impression of a runaway train or a bursting dam as Doris Brinkley went on.

"She was too self-conscious and empty-headed. Her characters lacked definition and were unconvincing. Insubstantial, really."

On a hunch, Rosa said, "We know you wrote those bad reviews." Out of the corner of her eye, she saw Miguel's eyebrows go up in surprise.

Miss Brinkley stammered. "I . . . w-what do you mean?"

"My cousin Gloria works at *The Santa Bonita Morning Star*," Rosa said, going further out on the limb. "She tells me that the entertainment editor has noticed that there are certain derogatory fan reviews that appear to come from another actress. I've had the opportunity to read a few."

Doris Brinkley appeared to be out of words.

Rosa quoted Miss Brinkley back to herself. "*Self-conscious and empty-headed. Unconvincing. Insubstantial.* The scathing reviewer used these exact terms. It was you who wrote those reviews, wasn't it?"

"Yes, all right. I wrote those reviews!" Miss Brinkley's face turned volcanic red. "Why should Charlene get all the good roles? I was always a better actress than her. She was all blond curls and round curves but nothing in here!" She tapped her chest above her heart. "I was sick of watching it. I felt I needed to speak for all struggling actresses like myself who constantly got bypassed because of prima donnas like Charlene Winters!"

She stopped suddenly and looked at Rosa and Miguel as if realizing, in a flash, what she had just confessed to.

"I'm so sorry!" Doris Brinkley's eyes welled with tears. She reached into her purse for a tissue. Rosa couldn't tell if Miss Brinkley was acting or being sincere. Clearly, Miss Brinkley was a better actress than Charlene Winters. However, that wouldn't help her in prison.

17

Miguel needed to return to his desk to attend to paperwork, and Rosa thought it an excellent time to return to her office and had Miguel drop her off there. She'd only been living in Santa Bonita for a few weeks when she opened her own investigative office. There was a certain thrill she still experienced in seeing her name embossed on the door: Rosa Reed Investigations.

On the second floor, the office window looked out to Main Street. Rosa set the satchel on the floor, and Diego languidly stepped out and made his way to his perch to look out the window. Rosa had outfitted the office with Scandinavian-style furniture, sparse yet efficient, inviting but not so much that a client would be tempted to overstay. In the adjoining kitchenette, Rosa put a kettle on for tea, then checked the mail that had been slipped through the slot in the door.

Nothing exceptional in the pile of envelopes: Advertisements for business services she didn't need, the latest *LIFE* magazine with a picture of a U.S. Airforce Vertijet taking off—its vertical position unbelievable—dominating the cover, and a bill for the electricity. Not too surprising since she'd only been away from her office for a couple of days. When the kettle whistle blew, Rosa prepared her tea and returned to her desk. She picked up the receiver of her black rotary telephone and dialed the numbers for the temp service she'd hired to check in with when she and Miguel had planned to be away. She wouldn't be needing their help now.

Would she?

Perhaps she should hire a receptionist to answer the telephone and make appointments. Gloria used to do that for her, but now her job at the newspaper took up all her time.

Just when she was about to ring the temp service, there was a knock on the door. Through the frosted-glass window, Rosa could make out the form of a man, slender and on the short side. As a woman who worked alone, Rosa took comfort in the fact that other businesses shared space on the same floor, and a scream would go a long way should she feel endangered. But rather than a sense of fear, this silhouette brought joy. She swung the door open.

"Scout!"

Scout removed his hat before stepping inside. "I was hoping I'd catch you."

"Come in," Rosa said, ushering her brother inside.

Scout glanced about the office with interest. "So, this is where you work?"

"Yes. Though I don't spend an awful lot of time here."

Stepping to the window, Scout peered out to the street. "Such wide roads," he mused. "I say, they have a lot of space here in America."

"Indeed," Rosa agreed with a grin.

Scout patted Diego on the head then turned to Rosa. "Aunt Louisa gave me instructions for getting here, kindly lending me a rather fabulous auto."

"Aunt Louisa is nothing if not a good hostess."

Scout shook the car keys in the air. "Shall we go for luncheon together?"

"What a fabulous idea!" Rosa gathered her purse and gloves, then took Scout's arm. "I know the perfect place, especially if you're driving a fabulous car."

Scout might've been an ace with horses, but Rosa held on to the handle of the Chevrolet Bel Air with white knuckles. She remembered belatedly that her brother wasn't exactly a proficient driver in England, reminding her much of her mother Ginger's driving prowess. So managing to steer a big machine while seated on the left and driving in the right lane was a major feat! Aunt Louisa had been generous in lending the yellow-and-white beauty, but Rosa felt that perhaps it would be best for them all and the Bel Air if she drove home.

Even so, she nervously gave instructions, guiding Scout safely onto Cedar Street and to the Steak & Shake. When the flamingo-pink restaurant appeared, Scout slammed on the brakes. "Now that's cooking with gas!"

"Keep driving," Rosa encouraged. "You don't want traffic to back up behind us."

Scout rolled the Bel Air into one of the parking stalls arranged in a semicircle.

As a waitress skillfully roller-skated to the driver's window, Scout stared at her in wonderment.

Rosa laughed. "You have to wind the window down."

Scout hurried to do the obvious, and the waitress grinned. "Can I take your order?"

"Well, erm, I don't know," Scout said, his accent a crisp contrast to the waitress' American counterpart. "What do you suggest?"

The waitress stared back, wide-eyed. "You're from England!"

"Indeed," Scout returned in amusement.

"Golly, I haven't met a real Englishman before."

"It's my pleasure to be your first, madam."

Rosa thought she'd better intervene before the poor woman's knees melted and her roller skates gave out from underneath her. She leaned over and spoke loudly. "We'll have two cheeseburgers, two orders of French fries, and two vanilla milkshakes, please."

Apparently, not as impressed by Rosa's English accent, the waitress scribbled the order on her notepad, smiled at Scout, and rolled away.

"Hunky-dory," Scout said cheerily. He stared at Rosa with appreciation. "I think I understand the appeal. Granted, Miguel's a decent bloke, but I didn't think any fellow would be worth giving up jolly old England for. If it weren't for Marvin, perhaps I'd move here myself."

Rosa doubted anything would pull Scout away from his beloved horse stables, even if it weren't for his cousin Marvin.

"How is Marvin?" she asked. "I didn't get to Bray Manor last time I was home."

"He's well. Still not much of a talker, but a good worker, so long as he doesn't need to depend on his left side."

Marvin Elliot had been in a shooting incident when Rosa was an infant, so she'd only ever known the man as somewhat feeble of mind and body. When Scout had set up his stud farm to breed race horses at Bray Manor in Hertfordshire, he took Marvin with him, giving him simple jobs and a good life.

The waitress rolled up to Scout's window and hooked a tray onto it. He insisted on paying, "Must relieve myself of this funny money," and handed Rosa her share of the meal.

After a few bites and a sip of his milk shake, Scout glanced at Rosa in appreciation. "Rather scrumptious!"

"This is the real reason I've moved here," Rosa said with a tease. "Don't tell Miguel."

"Your secret is safe with me, little sister."

Rosa considered Scout with affection. "I want to apologize for having been so busy since you arrived. We've hardly seen each other."

"There's no need to apologize. If things had gone the way we'd first expected, you'd be long gone already on your second honeymoon." He grinned at her. "I'm getting more than I bargained for and a grand hamburger as well. Besides, Clarence has been keeping me entertained.

Rosa didn't want to know what that meant and popped a French fry into her mouth as an excuse not to ask.

"How is your case going?" Scout said between

bites. "Are you and your detective husband getting closer to catching the killer?"

Rosa thought about the two interviews she and Miguel had had that morning with Hank Brummel and Doris Brinkley and grimaced. "Not really," she admitted. "But we'll keep investigating until we do."

Scout grinned. "You two really are like Mum and Dad. That's just the kind of thing she'd say."

Rosa smiled back. "I couldn't imagine a nicer compliment, Scout. Thank you."

18

The longer it took to capture a killer, the more likely the case would grow cold. Sitting in the driver's seat of her Corvette, Rosa tapped the steering wheel restlessly. While working for London's Metropolitan Police, she'd learned that it never hurt to revisit the crime scene, especially if the investigation slowed to a grind. Before joining the flow of the Santa Bonita traffic, she signaled and headed toward St. Francis' church.

It was a Tuesday morning, and the parking lot was empty. Rosa wondered if she was on a fool's errand. The church door was open, and she stepped inside the vestibule and then into the sanctuary, where she touched a sponge dampened with holy water and crossed herself. Even though she remained Protestant, she engaged in the practice as a sign of respect. She'd attended mass several times since she and Miguel had returned from London and accepted that she'd be attending an endless number more.

A door to the left opened, and Rosa glimpsed a nun wearing a full habit. Rosa smiled as she recognized the sister's perpetually cheery face. "Sister Evangeline."

"Oh, hello," the nun said as she approached. Sister Evangeline was the jovial type who wouldn't hurt a flea and immediately thought the best of everyone. Rosa found her well suited for her vocation.

"I thought I heard someone." Sister Evangeline squinted at Rosa, smiling wider as recognition hit. "Miss Reed? Or shall I say Mrs. Belmonte!" Her smile faltered briefly. "Shouldn't you and your new husband be off on a romantic honeymoon?"

"Our plans have been delayed," Rosa said. "But we will be shortly."

"Oh yes, the . . ." Sister Evangeline grimaced as she whispered. ". . . murder. Such a dreadful affair, and to happen on your wedding day. Such a shame."

Rosa thought of it as Bill and Carlotta's wedding day, thankful that she and Miguel had already had an uneventful wedding and honeymoon. "No one could've anticipated the sad event," she said.

Sister Evangeline clasped her hands together. "I should say not. Now, dear, I am afraid Father Navarro is visiting the sick. Is there something I can do for you?"

"I'm not sure," Rosa answered truthfully. "I wonder if I could see the reception hall and kitchen again. I know it's a strange request..."

"Oh, you want to return to the crime scene." Sister Evangeline's eyes sparkled. "Don't tell anyone, but I do enjoy a good Agatha Christie or Dorothy L. Sayers once in a while."

Rosa followed Sister Evangeline across the foyer to the reception hall. "I regret missing your nuptials," the sister started, "but my service at the Holy Mother's Hand of Hope was needed."

Rosa was aware of the charity through another recent case and respected the sisters' work to assist girls in need. "How is it going at the Hand of Hope?" she asked.

"Busy, busy, busy. A lot of Mexican immigrants come into California, and many of them are girls in distress. Thankfully, we have the help of volunteers. I don't know what I'd do without people like Mr. and Mrs. Pérez." She eyed Rosa in a hopeful way, but Rosa stayed quiet.

As much as she'd like to, Rosa didn't have the time to volunteer anywhere at the moment.

Sister Evangeline added, "The Pérezes are retired, so they have the time. They have made it their mission to spend their senior years helping newcomers settle."

The sister glanced briefly at her wristwatch, and

Rosa said, "I'm fine to meander on my own if that's all right with you."

"Are you sure?" Sister Evangeline asked. "I did have a few things that need to be attended to, but I don't want you to feel I've abandoned you."

"Not at all," Rosa said encouragingly. She'd rather be alone with her thoughts. "I won't be long. Just a few minutes. I can see myself out."

"Very well. It's a pleasure to see you again, Mrs. Belmonte. Since you haven't left on your honeymoon, I'll see you on Sunday?"

Rosa nodded. "That is quite likely."

"God bless you." Sister Evangeline held her palms together as if in prayer and then left.

The reception hall was cleared of all the tables, and the chairs were folded and leaning against the wall near the stage. It was eerily quiet, and Rosa's mind flashed memories of the vibrant celebrations—everyone eating, drinking, laughing, and dancing. Miguel serenading her from the stage—Sister Evangeline was right. The sudden stop to the happy time was a shame.

Rosa returned to the spot where she'd been standing when the waitress had screamed out. She'd been facing the stage but had turned toward the commotion. Her feet had moved before she'd had a chance to think, and she was one of the first to see what had elicited the terror—Charlene's pale arm hanging limply from the bottom of the serving trolley.

Returning to the kitchen, Rosa walked through what she could imagine was Charlene's last moment. Starting in the bathroom at the back, she took a moment to look in the mirror. Her reflection was opposite of what she remembered Charlene looked like: Rosa had dark hair, and Charlene's was bleached blond. Rosa's eyes were green compared with Charlene's darker tones. And Rosa's teardrop face contrasted with Charlene's round one.

Exhaling, Rosa stepped back into the hallway. She had two choices to get back to the reception hall. Turn right at the adjoining hall linking to the foyer, then enter through the main doors or go straight past the kitchen. The latter was intrusive for the kitchen staff but would take less time. Was Charlene in a hurry to get back to the party? Had she heard Miguel's band playing? Or was she simply unconcerned about whether she'd inconvenience anyone?

Whatever her reasoning, she'd chosen to go straight through the kitchen. Her attacker must've been waiting in the adjoining hallway. Had they argued? Was that why Charlene didn't take the long way back to the reception hall?

Perhaps, after the argument, Charlene had headed through the kitchen and turned her back on her nemesis. A frying pan, left on the counter, was in view and within reach. In a moment of fury, the killer picked it up and struck Charlene on the head.

Rosa lifted a frying pan hanging from a row of pot hooks, similar in size and weight to the one in evidence, and mimicked the motion. The cast iron was heavy and required a good deal of strength to wield. She could hardly imagine someone like Doris Brinkley pulling it off.

After returning the frying pan, Rosa left the church feeling like she'd accomplished little.

19

*R*osa and Miguel arrived home at nearly the same time.

"Hello, beautiful," Miguel said as he greeted Rosa with a kiss.

"Hello, handsome," she returned.

Diego had made himself at home in an armchair, and Rosa reached over to pat his neck. "Hello, lazy boy. Now, why don't you have dinner on?"

Diego stared blankly at Rosa, then rose to his haunches. But instead of jumping to the floor to run a figure eight between her legs, he licked his paw and drew it over his forehead.

"It's dinnertime, not bath time." Rosa laughed. It was almost 6 p.m., and Rosa was hungry. She imagined Miguel was too. She looked at her husband, who watched her. The reality of being a wife with little domestic experience and a busy schedule touched down like an airplane on a runway.

"I'm sorry," she said after a beat. "Was I meant to make dinner?"

"It is the natural way of things," Miguel said, then quickly added, "but have no fear!" As he disappeared into the kitchen, Rosa sat on the couch and took off her shoes.

A moment later, Miguel appeared in the kitchen doorway with a small, flat package in each hand and held them up. Rosa made out the words "Swanson TV Dinner" amidst the graphic that looked like little television sets with dials and a screen showing some kind of food.

"I love these things," Miguel said with a grin. "The food is precooked and placed in tin trays, each food item separated from the others. You put them in your freezer and take them out when you want to have a meal. It only takes a half hour to cook if the oven is warmed up first."

Rosa had tried them once before when visiting Nancy and understood the appeal, but nothing could come close to the delight Señora Gomez's cooking brought to the senses.

"A big help for the working man," Miguel continued, ". . . or woman." He held the frozen dinners up so Rosa could see the photographed image of what was apparently inside. "Would you like Salisbury steak or turkey?"

"A hard choice," Rosa said, wishing there was a third, fresher option.

"They both have mashed potatoes, gravy, and peas, but the turkey has apple cobbler for dessert. The Salisbury has . . ." He looked at the picture. "Something . . . else."

"Turkey, please."

"I'll turn the oven on," he said cheerfully.

But Rosa could tell he was hoping for the apple cobbler for himself.

Rosa relaxed into Miguel's leather easy chair. It felt just a bit lumpy, and Rosa mentally noted that it probably needed to be replaced soon. Her favorite lounge chair at the Forrester house always felt firm, and sometimes one could even detect the faint smell of the vinegar-and-water solution used to clean it.

This one smelled musty.

"Satisfying and delicious!"

Rosa spun to Homer's voice from inside his cage, suspended by a chain from a hook in the ceiling. The parrot squawked, then buried his beak under his wing. Diego instantly crouched low to the ground and glided across the floor before jumping onto the table, bringing him to the same level as the bird. He ducked his furry head, his eyes fastening on Homer, who seemed to pay him no attention.

"Fearsome hunter," Rosa said as she watched, wondering if she should intervene and save the poor bird from getting a fright.

Miguel stood in the kitchen doorway with one finger on his lips and whispered, "Watch."

Diego's tail swished as his body shimmied, his eyes never leaving the hanging cage containing his unsuspecting prey. There was no way for Diego to get close enough to even touch the outside of the cage without launching himself through about six feet of empty air space between table and cage. But for reasons Rosa found unfathomable, Diego didn't seem to think that was an issue.

Rosa watched in mute fascination as her cat, still crouched, wiggled his furry bottom to prepare for lift off.

Homer suddenly shrieked, "Bang! You're dead, hombre!"

Startled, Diego leaped sideways off the table, displacing the tablecloth and upending a bowl. He scrambled under a chair where he stopped to look back at the cage with all the fur on his tail puffed up and his ears flattened.

"It never gets old!" Miguel said with a laugh. Carrying two bottles of Mexican beer into the room, he added, "Deputy Diego is pretty smart for a cat, but man, that loco bird gets him every time. Since I watched that western on TV last month, Homer has been saying that phrase repeatedly."

"Jolly good entertainment." Rosa giggled. "Oh, Diego, did Homer scare you?"

Diego licked his lips and lay down on his stomach under the chair.

"Right now, he's saying, well played, you little *diablo*," Miguel said. "But I will get you next time." He laughed as he handed a bottle to Rosa and sat on the sofa.

"All right," Miguel said, taking a long sip and leaning back. "I've been looking forward to the typical husband and wife conversations. I'll start. How was your day, my dear?"

Although Rosa wasn't used to drinking beer straight from the bottle, she didn't feel like searching for a glass. She took a small sip, then said, "You go first."

"Okay, my big news of the day is that we can probably take Hank Brummel off the suspect list."

"Oh?" Rosa said. "That is rather disappointing."

"Why is that?"

"He lied to his wife and put another woman in the family way. I'm afraid I don't have a soft spot for the man."

"I take your point." Miguel raised his bottle. "But he is a cop. I'm pleased a fellow officer didn't commit the crime."

"That's true," Rosa conceded. "So, why are we taking him off the list?"

"Because he did make a call from the church payphone while Charlene was being murdered. We finally tracked down records from that day. A call was made to Marjorie Brummel in Los Angeles."

"Oh, that man!" Rosa scowled. "Checking in with his wife while on a date with another woman."

"He may be a cad, but he's not a stone-cold killer." Miguel caught Rosa's eye and inclined his head. "How was your afternoon?"

"I decided to call in at the church hall this afternoon, you know, to revisit the crime scene, poke around a bit."

"Did you discover anything new?"

"No, but I had an enjoyable conversation with Sister Evangeline, a very lovely nun. We discussed immigration, and she told me about an older couple that has made it their mission to help newcomers get settled—the Pérezes."

"Oh, yes," Miguel said. "Julio and Isabella Pérez. Everyone at the church knows who they are."

"Aunt Louisa is involved in charity work. She's probably aware of them too."

"I wonder if they helped Alicia Rodriguez?" Miguel said.

Rosa shot him a puzzled look. "What brought that up?"

"Well, she's one of the few people without a proper alibi," Miguel said. "We can't let the fact that she's employed by your cousin keep us from doing our due diligence."

Before Rosa could respond, the timer in the kitchen rang. Miguel jumped to his feet. "You set up the TV trays, and I'll get the dinners. I think Perry Mason is on soon."

Miguel returned with the dinners and placed them on the TV trays. They finished eating just as Perry Mason was making his case to the jury, but before they could watch the final outcome, they were interrupted by a knock at the door.

"I'm not expecting anyone," Miguel said. "Are you?"

"No," Rosa said as Miguel got up to answer it.

"Hello, you two!" Gloria's cheerful voice rang through the entrance. "I thought I would stop by on my way home."

Rosa stood to greet her cousin. "This is a surprise! Come on in."

Gloria entered the small living room and scanned it. Rosa could only imagine she was comparing it with the vastness of the Forrester mansion, the only home she had ever known. "Very quaint," she said. "Maybe I should get myself a little house like this. Something Mom wouldn't dream of stepping foot in."

She laughed then stared back at Rosa with a look of horror. "Oh, that didn't come out well."

Rosa grinned. "It's all right. There's something to be said about small and peaceful." She motioned to the couch. "Please have a seat."

"Thank you," Gloria said, sitting.

"Can I get you a drink?" Miguel offered. "I'm afraid there's not a lot on offer. Beer or Coca-Cola."

"I'll take the soda," Gloria said. "I'm quite parched." Her eyes moved about the room and landed on the bird cage. She pointed. "Is that bird real?"

Homer seemed intent on clarifying. He screeched, "Va-va-voom!" Gloria burst out laughing.

Rosa looked suspiciously at Miguel as he returned with Gloria's drink. "Where did he learn that phrase?"

"Must've been from before I got him." Miguel shrugged, but he couldn't hide a smirk.

Rosa turned back to Gloria. "That's Homer. He's the African gray parrot I told you about. He can be a bit cheeky."

"Keen!" Gloria said. She sipped her soda and then added, "I'm here on business. I've got juicy news on

Mr. Sussman, and I knew you'd want to hear about it immediately."

Rosa leaned in. "Do tell."

"It turns out the New National Theater Coalition was holding a seminar this afternoon at the Santa Monica Art House, so I attended."

"You did?" Rosa was impressed at her cousin's investigative tenacity.

"Yes, it was an open-to-the-public event. The guest speaker was some famous Argentinian playwright."

"Did he happen to be from Buenos Aires?" Rosa asked.

Gloria nodded. "Yes. He spoke on Stanislavski's method of acting, but here's the interesting part." Gloria's eyes lit up with excitement. "There was another reporter, a woman journalist from *The Santa Monica Gazette*. I saw her taking notes and snapping pictures and felt she might be a reporter. I started a conversation with her, and we ended up having a coffee at a nearby café. She told me that she had been investigating the NNTC for quite some time. She had a lot of information about it and other organizations like it across the States." She stopped and stared at them, looking like she was about to burst.

"I feel like you are about to drop a bombshell on us," Miguel said.

"Communists!" Gloria shouted as she raised both

hands in the air and then let them drop onto her lap with a hard slapping sound. "Those guys are all communists!"

Rosa and Miguel shared a look of astonishment.

"The NNTC, in particular, has strong ties to the communist movement in Argentina," Gloria continued. "Their goal is to mentor and influence actors, academics, intellectuals, playwrights, directors, and other people in the world of the arts and academia who might someday become sympathetic to the cause of communism and become cultural opinion-makers."

"Agents of influence," Rosa said. "I've read about that. These people use their position of influence and celebrity to subliminally change culture in the West more towards Marxist philosophy."

Miguel whistled. "Like spies?"

"Not exactly," Rosa said. "Spies are ordered directly by their governments. These agents of influence are almost totally autonomous from any direct influence of the KGB, FBI or anything like that."

"Eisenhower outlawed the Communist Party a few years ago," Miguel said.

"That's why everything is so hush-hush," Gloria said.

"If this was found to be true and proven," Miguel added thoughtfully, "there would be many arrests."

"Proving it would be hard to do with such shadowy

and loosely connected organizations like NNTC," Rosa returned.

"The influence of these communist fronts also extends into the world of journalism," Gloria added. "That's why this reporter from *The Gazette* was on the case. Her boss's plan was for her to find out everything she could and for the newspaper to blow it all open."

"So, Donald Sussman might be a communist," Miguel said.

"At the very least, he may be one of these agents-of-influence chaps." Rosa wrinkled her nose. "He could've been pressuring Charlene."

"And if she resisted, or worst threatened to expose him—" Miguel started.

Rosa finished his thought. "He might've decided to stop her."

20

The next morning Miguel guided Rosa's Corvette along the paved, winding road and up the rolling hills north of town toward Rancho Bonito Winery. Aunt Louisa had highly recommended visiting the vineyard before, and Rosa wanted to see the place. She hadn't imagined that it would be a murder investigation that would finally bring her to the sprawling two-hundred-acre property.

"Beautiful," Miguel said appreciatively.

"Yes," Rosa agreed. "It's a wonderful view."

"I'm talking about this thing," Miguel said, tapping his hands on the red-leather-covered steering wheel.

Considering the prestigious destination and the scenic drive involved, Miguel had suggested taking the Corvette and that he, rather than Rosa, should drive the car. The road took them through acres and acres of vineyards almost as far as the eye could see.

Rosa held a hand on the scarf covering her hair. Riding in a convertible was fun, but the Pacific breeze messed up a good hairdo.

"We have wineries in England too," she said.

Miguel stared back with disbelief flashing in his eyes. "I don't recall seeing any when I was there. I thought that was the domain of Italy and France."

"Certainly, the Continent has more to offer in the way of vineyards and wineries, but there are a few small ones in the south of England; however, they don't look quite like this."

The road ended near the top of a wide hill in a large parking lot about half full. One had to climb a long flight of wooden stairs to reach the beautiful Spanish colonial-style building that housed a bistro and several wine tasting rooms. The view of the valley from that height was breathtaking.

Donald Sussman sat at a round table covered with a red-linen cloth and dotted with plates of assorted cheeses, grapes, and slices of artisan bread. There was a bottle of red wine and a nearly empty wineglass near his right hand. He grinned when he saw them. They were expected.

"Ah, there you are," Mr. Sussman said as he rose to

shake Rosa and Miguel's hands. "You found the place okay?"

"We did," Miguel said. "Thanks for your directions and your willingness to meet."

"I couldn't very well say no to the police," he said with a strained chuckle. "Business brought me here. I appreciate you coming this way." He raised the bottle on the table. "This is a very nice Bordeaux. You'll have to try some."

"Unfortunately, I'm on duty," Miguel said.

"Of course," Mr. Sussman said, then looked at Rosa.

"I'm fine for now as well," she said.

"Well, there are excellent sandwiches if you crave more than these nibbles on the table."

Rosa glanced around the establishment, its theme of wine and vines evident in the decor. "Is this place of special interest to you?"

"Guilty as charged," Mr. Sussman chuckled like a man without a care. "I might invest in this place. Wine is big business, and good wine is great business."

"Do you have experience in winemaking?" Rosa asked.

Mr. Sussman smirked. "None at all. But I'm a man who likes to try new things, and when I found this opportunity, I made a few calls." He raised his glass again and slowly rolled the wine around before putting it back on the table.

"Good legs," Miguel said, nodding at how the wine coursed down the sides of the glass in thick rivulets. Rosa glanced at her husband in surprise. She had no idea Miguel knew the first thing about wine.

"I'll say," Donald Sussman said coarsely, his eyes lingering on Rosa's ankles. Miguel cleared his throat in disapproval.

"You must know we didn't come to talk about wine," she said. "As lovely as it is here."

Mr. Sussman lifted a shoulder before taking a sip of his wine. "Of course," he said languidly. "I'm not a fool."

Gone was the impatient chap they had first interviewed after the murder occurred. Surely, Mr. Sussman realized that the police still considered him a suspect if there was a follow-up interview. She questioned his seemingly tranquil and polished composure, believing it to be an act—and a high caliber one at that. Not bad coming from someone who claimed he wasn't an actor.

"We would like to talk to you more about this organization you mentioned," Miguel started. "The New National Theater Coalition."

"Again, you're surprising me with your line of questioning, Detective," Mr. Sussman said coyly.

"What on earth has that got to do with the murder investigation?"

"Because we've been told that you were trying to recruit Charlene Winters," Miguel said.

"And I *told* you, she wasn't interested, and that was that."

"Why do you suppose she wasn't interested?" Miguel asked. "She was an actress, and the organization pandered to the creative type."

"I don't know," Mr. Sussman returned with a huff. "She said she didn't have time."

"Are you a communist?" Rosa asked, cutting to the chase. "Is that why Miss Winters turned you down? Were you hoping she would become an agent of influence for your cause?"

Donald Sussman slowly put his wine glass on the table and sighed heavily. He leaned forward with an elbow on the table and, with his other hand, absentmindedly tapped his temple with two fingers. Finally, he said, "Are you two nuts?"

"Were you afraid Miss Winters would expose your communist ties?" Miguel asked.

"What is this?" Mr. Sussman blustered. "The McCarthy hearings are over, haven't you heard?"

"I'm not a politician, Mr. Sussman," Miguel said, "but I do know that if word spread that NNTC had ties to red organizations, maybe in places like

Argentina, your group would lose its influence very quickly. Most folks in Santa Bonita still have a healthy distaste for anything communist, as do most Americans. Just think, all your hard work down the drain if the truth were known."

"You saw Miss Winters leave her seat at our reception," Rosa added, "perhaps thinking you would have a word with her in private. One last chance to talk some sense into her."

"But it turned into an argument," Miguel added. "Miss Winters refused to help you and maybe even threatened to bring you down."

A server from the bistro, a young man wearing black trousers and a crisp white shirt, stepped up to the table. "Sorry to disturb you, Mr. Sussman, but there is an urgent phone call for you. You can take it in the office behind the bistro."

"Thank you," Mr. Sussman said as he slowly got up, still the perfect picture of calm and cool. Smoothing out his suit jacket, he faced Rosa and Miguel. "I really think you two should order a glass of wine. It might calm your thinking a little, and then we can talk with level heads when I get back."

"He's a smooth one, isn't he?" Miguel said to Rosa as they watched the man disappear.

Rosa drummed her fingers on the table. "He's lying."

"I think so too."

After a few minutes of staring at the captivating view, Rosa glanced at the sliding glass doors that Donald Sussman had disappeared through. "I'm getting suspicious." Standing, she headed toward the bistro area, Miguel on her heels. It took a moment to find the waiter that had come out to them on the veranda.

As they approached him, Rosa said, "Excuse me, but we need to talk to Mr. Sussman immediately. Could you please direct us to where he is using the phone?"

"I . . . I'm not sure . . ."

Miguel pulled out his police identification. "This is a police matter, and it's urgent."

The waiter's eyes grew round. He lifted a palm. "Hey there, I don't want any trouble. The police, oh man."

"Then tell us where he is," Rosa said.

"I don't rightly know. He gave me this signal, see? Two fingers tapping on his temple. If I saw that, I was supposed to tell him about a fake phone call." He pulled a face, then added, "He paid me ten bucks."

Miguel let out a breath of frustration. "Which way did he go?"

"Out to the parking lot." The waiter shrugged sheepishly. "I think he's gone."

Rosa and Miguel rushed out the front entrance. From there, one could see parts of the winding road far below as it snaked down to the coast. Miguel pointed to a blue car, now looking about the size of an ant, pulling onto the coast highway heading south. "That's probably him."

Even with Rosa's Corvette, there was no way they could catch him.

Blast it.

21

Miguel phoned the police station, triggering an all-points bulletin on Donald Sussman. He and Rosa then headed back to the police station. Rosa glanced at the speedometer, wondering if she should mention her husband's lead foot. The speed limit was posted, and he was the police.

She placed a hand on Miguel's arm and said, "Darling, I'd like to get back in one piece."

Miguel seemed to snap out of his state of anxious frustration long enough to release pressure on the accelerator.

"Sorry, my dear. I'm just angry at myself for getting duped."

"We had no reason to suspect duplicity," Rosa said, though she was feeling rather cross at herself as well.

"But I'm sure the department will find and apprehend him in time." Again, Rosa wasn't as certain as she claimed. Slippery men like Donald Sussman had a way of escaping the law and their due justice. But one could hope.

"While you're doing your job at the precinct," Rosa said, "I think I'll have a chat with Aunt Louisa. Perhaps she knows something that will give us a clue where Mr. Sussman might hide."

Miguel agreed this would be a good next step, so when they arrived at the Santa Bonita Police Station, Rosa moved into the driver's spot. Miguel kissed her before she left.

"Let me know what you find out," he said.

"I will."

"I mean it, Rosa. If your aunt knows where Sussman is, call me. What happened to Charlene? Well, I can't lose you like that."

"I'll be careful, Miguel," Rosa said. "I promise. If you'll do the same."

Miguel kissed her again, speaking as his lips touched hers. "I promise."

As she drove away, Rosa's fingers went to her lips. She prayed she'd never take Miguel's love for granted. Her work as an investigator had improved since teaming up with him, but it also put her on her back foot with constant worry and concern. She supposed that came with the territory of being married to a police officer. On the other hand, Miguel had taken on the same risks by marrying her instead of someone contented to stay home and warm the hearth.

Miguel could've chosen a traditional American bride, and perhaps he would've been better off in the long run, but then again, her mother and father had made a fine pair. Ginger and Basil Reed had worked many cases together, and from the stories she'd heard, some had been precarious! The apple hadn't fallen far from the tree with Rosa, first becoming a police constable, following in her father's footsteps, and then, after arriving in Santa Bonita, setting up an investigative office like her mother.

These were her thoughts as she steered her Corvette down the long palm-tree-lined drive to Forrester mansion, and by the time she'd parked, she felt much better. She and Miguel would do just fine.

Rosa paused at the front door. When she'd lived there, she naturally never knocked before entering, but now that she was no longer a resident, she was unsure. Still, she was family. She decided that knocking while opening the door and announcing her arrival was a fine way to deal with the conundrum.

"Hello? It's me, Rosa. Anyone home?"

Gloria appeared, stepping into the entrance way

from the door leading to the living room. "Rosa! We're in here. Watching *Lassie* with Grandma Sally."

The living room at the Forrester mansion had a Scandinavian-style low-back, aqua-blue section couch with matching chairs. This set faced a glass-topped coffee table positioned on a yellow rug. The heavy drapes—yellow embossed with a white geometrical pattern—were opened, letting in the seemingly endless sunlight.

"Hi, Grandma Sally, Aunt Louisa," Rosa said. She was happy to see her family gathered, though she'd hoped to speak to her aunt alone.

"Hello, Rosa," Aunt Louisa said. "The show is just finishing up. There's a carafe of hot coffee if you're interested."

"Thank you," Rosa said. "I am." She poured for herself and added a little sugar before claiming one of the empty chairs.

Rosa joined in with the TV-watching until, once again, Lassie saved the day. The ending credits came up with the theme song, and everyone stretched and readied to leave. Rosa motioned to her aunt. "Actually, I came over to speak to you, Aunt Louisa."

Aunt Louisa stood and smoothed out her skirt. "I'll be in my office when you've finished your coffee. I've got March of Dimes coming up and so many details to attend to."

"Is Scout around?" Rosa asked. "I've been neglecting him terribly."

"Oh, I wouldn't worry about him," Gloria said with a chuckle. "Clarence is determined to make an American out of him before he leaves. They're doing everything from eating apple pie to going to baseball games to shooting at the gun range."

Rosa smiled. "He's definitely having more fun with Clarence than he would with me."

"It's good to see Clarence keeping busy," Grandma Sally said.

Where Aunt Louisa seemed ageless, Grandma Sally Hartigan seemed forever elderly. Rosa couldn't remember her looking any other way. Soft, wrinkled skin, white hair pulled back in a bun, and a bent-over posture robbing her of height.

"He was moping about so much I wanted to call him Eeyore," Grandma Sally continued. "I'm glad to see his preoccupation with that nanny has been diverted." With some effort, she pushed herself to her feet. Rosa nearly jumped to assist, even though Grandma Sally had made it clear she didn't like to be treated like an old lady. "He needs to find a suitable wife, and mother for Julie," Grandma Sally continued, "and the sooner the better."

"I really should go too," Gloria said once Grandma Sally had left the room. "I promised Jake I'd come by the newspaper and read over some of his copy."

"Please don't change your plans on my account," Rosa said, standing. She placed her empty coffee cup back on the tray. "I'm not planning to stay long."

"How is the case going?" Gloria asked. "Did you find Donald Sussman?"

"We did," Rosa said. "And he behaved very suspiciously indeed, but it doesn't mean he's our killer. Which reminds me, how well do you know Doris Brinkley? You spent a good amount of time together when you were an aspiring actress, is that not so?"

Gloria shrugged. "I suppose. There were a lot of girls trying to break in at the time. I doubt that's changed. Why?"

"She claims to have been in the restroom when Miss Winters was killed—with stomach ailments. However, there's no one to verify her story."

"Stomach ailments, huh?" Gloria said with a grimace. "Right after eating dinner at your reception. My bet is she was making herself sick."

"Why would she do that?" Rosa asked.

"To keep from gaining weight from the food. It's quite common in the industry with young actresses, I'm afraid," Gloria said. "The pressure to have an impossibly tiny waist is real. I know Doris does it. I caught her once myself."

Rosa felt for the young actress and wouldn't have been surprised if Gloria's guess was correct. Miss Brinkley seemed the type to do anything to follow her dreams of being a great actress. That could also even be to the point of trying to sabotage her competition, which didn't absolve her from killing for the same reasons.

22

Aunt Louisa was in her office, at her desk. She was on the telephone with her back to the door. Assuming her aunt was talking to other charity organizers, Rosa quietly sat on the sofa. She'd learned from attending other charity events that there were many details to consider: booking venues, catering, parking, bands, prizes, and other incentives for people to open their pocketbooks.

"It's not that I don't want to see you again, Elliot..."

Suddenly aware that her aunt's call was personal, Rosa blushed. Should she slip out and announce her "arrival" with a firm throat-clearing? Or better yet, wait in the hallway until her aunt had ended her call? But could she manage an escape without her aunt knowing she'd been listening?

"It's complicated. I'm just swamped now."

Oh dear. The longer Rosa waited, the more unconvincing her excuses would be. She imagined not only her own embarrassment but that of her aunt as well. Why hadn't her aunt closed the door?

"Elliot, please. Can we discuss this later? My niece is waiting to speak to me."

Oh drat. Aunt Louisa had known all along. That explained her trying to hang up on poor rejected Mr. Roundtree.

Aunt Louisa returned the black receiver to its cradle and then faced Rosa with a blank expression. "You want to speak to me?"

"Yes," Rosa said, looking away as she adjusted the layers of her skirt. She pretended she hadn't overheard her aunt break the ranch manager's heart. "I wanted to ask you about your friend Mr. Sussman."

"Mr. Sussman is an acquaintance at best." Aunt Louisa narrowed her eyes. "Don't tell me you suspect him of killing that actress."

"He can't account for his whereabouts when Miss Winters was killed," Rosa said.

"What does he say about that?"

"That he went out for a cigarette."

"And you doubt that because?"

"The timing is rather convenient. And no one else

saw him, not even Officer Brummel, who was outside using the payphone."

"I see. Well, I don't know how I can help. I barely know the man."

Rosa had feared this. "Are you unaware of his affiliation to covert communist associations?"

Aunt Louisa scowled. "Don't tell me those rumors are true. I would've never let him step foot in my house had I known."

"We suspect he may have been trying to recruit Miss Winters," Rosa said. "Many people in Hollywood are suspected of being agents of influence for the communist cause."

Aunt Louisa huffed. "I suppose there will always be some dolt trying to poison the pot."

"Do you know where Mr. Sussman might go if he fancied hiding from the police?"

"I suppose if he were really in danger of going to prison, he might head back to Buenos Aires."

Rosa and Miguel had already discussed that possibility. If the police were going to stop the man, they'd have to check all the airports and border crossings.

Not wanting to keep her aunt longer than necessary, Rosa got to her feet. "Thank you, Aunt Louisa. If you hear from him, please let the police know immediately."

"Sure."

Rosa hesitated by the door.

"Is there something else, Rosa?" her aunt asked.

In general, Rosa made a point of minding her own business, but she wanted to make an exception with her aunt. After a breath, she said, "Uncle Harold has been gone for thirteen years, and in all that time, you've never met anyone who's made you feel the way Mr. Roundtree does. Aunt Louisa, you only live once. Why don't you let yourself be happy?"

If Rosa thought her aunt would soften and agree with her sentimentality, she was to be disappointed. Instead, Aunt Louisa straightened in her chair, her expression hardening. "If I wanted your advice on romantic matters, I would've said so. Now, please close the door on your way out."

Rosa chastised herself as she stepped out of the office. Her relationship with her aunt had never been smooth, and now she'd just dug new trenches between them. It'd ease again over time, that much Rosa knew from experience. Perhaps Aunt Louisa was happy, in her own stubborn sort of way.

Rosa wouldn't leave the Forrester mansion without saying a quick hello to Señora Gomez. Boisterous male voices reached her as she drew close to the kitchen. Scout and Clarence, seated in the morning room that overlooked the pool and its vast surrounding gardens, were enjoying cold drinks and discussing how they'd enjoyed their day so far.

"How nice to be gentlemen of leisure," Rosa said with a smile.

"Rosa!" Scout said. "Fancy meeting you here!"

"You must join us for a drink," Clarence said. "Freshly squeezed lemonade. Do you believe your brother has never had one?"

"I do," Rosa said, joining them. "One doesn't find lemon trees in England. And after the war, rationing seemed to go on forever, so there wasn't much sugar to be had either."

"Here, here, Miss Rosa," Señora Gomez said as she delivered a tall glass of cool lemonade to Rosa. "It is the best in Santa Bonita!"

Rosa didn't doubt it. "Thank you, Señora Gomez!"

"How is our perfect little kitten, Diego? Does he like his new *casa*?"

"He misses you, but he's adjusting," Rosa said. "Homer is good company."

"Homer?" Señora Gomez asked, her forehead breaking into several rows of wrinkles.

"Miguel's parrot," Rosa returned. "You wouldn't believe how chatty that bird is."

Señora Gomez seemed unimpressed. She looked displeased that a bird had taken her place as Diego's home-based companion.

Rosa hurried to encourage her. "But I can tell Diego misses you. I'll bring him for a visit soon."

The promise did its immediate work of brightening the housekeeper's countenance. "Gracias, Miss Rosa."

Turning back to her brother and cousin, Rosa asked, "So what have you two gentlemen been up to?"

"Yesterday, Clarence took me to a stock car race," Scout said. "In the evening, we went to a music event featuring . . . er . . ." he turned to Clarence. "What was the name of that guitar-playing chap?"

Clarence grinned crookedly. "Chet Atkins."

"Yes, that's it." Scout slapped his knee. "Brilliant music. Very American-sounding."

"We just got in from taking a couple of mom's horses out for a ride," Clarence said. "Scout here said he was swimming in the western-style saddle."

"It's bigger than I'm used to," Scout said.

Clarence laughed. "Everything is bigger in America."

"Yesterday, your cousin took me to a baseball game," Scout said. "Quaint."

"Scout keeps telling me about the differences in cricket," Clarence said. "I finally bought him a hotdog to shut him up."

"A delicious treat the hotdog was, indeed," Scout said, "if not a tad messy."

Rosa laughed. She could only imagine her brother

attempting to eat a hotdog without dripping the mustard.

"The ladies league is playing today," Clarence said. "Vanessa is dropping Julie off soon, so I thought we'd go."

Vanessa was Clarence's former wife. When they'd first separated, Julie lived nearly full time with her mother, but Vanessa started dropping her off more and leaving her for longer periods. Julie was with the Forrester family more often than not, which had prompted Clarence to hire a nanny.

"It would be fun for her to see her nanny play."

Rosa was surprised that her thoughts about the nanny came simultaneously with Clarence's words.

"Alicia is playing?"

Clarence looked away like the fact was no big deal, but the blush on his neck was telling. "Yeah, she's cookin', too."

Scout flashed Rosa a look of confusion. "What's she cooking?"

Rosa chuckled. "He means she's good at the game." Turning to her cousin, she added airily, "I'm curious, Clarence. How did you find Alicia? Surely you didn't put an ad in the papers."

Clarence snorted. "Of course not. Señora Gomez mentioned that a couple from her church placed housekeepers and nannies in homes. They had a good reputation. To be sure, I called other families who'd gotten nannies through their referrals. They sent Alicia, and I knew she'd be a good fit for Julie after our first interview."

"How nice," Rosa said. "What is the name of the couple? In case Miguel and I decide to get help around the house."

Her example was a ruse, as the Belmonte family and Mrs. Belmonte, in particular, frowned on hiring outside help. Rosa had been raised with a nanny and found such an arrangement helpful to both parties—they provided employment for someone looking to work and they had assistance with childcare. However, that would be a discussion she'd save to have with Miguel another day.

"Julio and Isabella Pérez," Clarence said.

Were they the same Pérezes that Sister Evangeline had talked about? Rosa asked her cousin, "Do you have an address or telephone number for them?"

"I'll get it for you." Clarence pushed away from the table, leaving Scout and Rosa alone in the morning room.

"Why don't you come with us?" Scout said. "I'd love to see you eat one of those hotdogs. It's rather barbaric eating with one's hands like that, yet quite liberating. Makes me feel rather at home, come to think of it."

Rosa chuckled. "While you're reverting to your childhood on the streets, I'm imagining Aunt Felicia attempting to eat one with a fork and knife."

That elicited a smile from Scout. "So? Will you come?"

Nothing would make Rosa happier, but first, she wanted to speak to Julio and Isabella Pérez.

"I have a short errand to run," Rosa said, "but why don't I meet you there."

Scout tipped an imaginary hat. "That would be splendid."

23

Julio and Isabella Pérez lived in a cozy apartment a few blocks from St. Francis Church. After declining a cup of hibiscus tea for the second time since arriving ten minutes prior, Rosa finally relented at Mrs. Pérez's third offer. She waited in the living room alone while Julio and Isabella fussed in the kitchen. Rosa almost felt like she was in a back room at the church. The walls were adorned with various examples of Catholic religious art, including a small crucifix, rosaries, and candles. But the most prominent piece of art was a huge painting of the Sacred Heart of Jesus. Rosa stared at the depiction of a Latino-looking Savior—as compared with the very pale versions found in the Church of England sanctuaries—dressed in purple and red robes, his head encircled by a halo. Streams of golden light emanated from his heart. His right hand was up as if in a friendly wave, and Rosa couldn't help but shyly slip her own hand up and give a small wave back.

"I am sure he appreciates the gesture, Señora," Julio said with a chuckle as he entered the room. He carried a plate of assorted cookies as his wife followed close behind with a tray carrying a decanter of tea and three ornately decorated teacups.

"It just seemed like the right thing to do," Rosa said, feeling a little embarrassed.

"You are not Catholic?" Mrs. Pérez earnestly asked as she put her tray on the coffee table and sat opposite Rosa on a brown leather armchair. She was a kind-looking lady in her mid-fifties with salt-and-pepper hair and olive skin. The couple were the quintessential opposites—Mrs. Pérez appeared no taller than five feet and rather soft, while her husband looked almost six feet tall and thin as a rail. They both spoke with heavy Spanish accents like so many people Rosa had gotten to know in Santa Bonita.

Rosa hesitated before answering her hostess' question. She didn't want to discuss her Protestant upbringing or that Mrs. Belmonte wished she'd convert to the Catholic faith.

"Of course, she is," Mr. Pérez said. "Do you think

Maria Belmonte would allow her to marry into the family without being Catholic?"

Rosa smiled with tight lips as she engaged in the sin of omission.

"I've heard your wedding was *muy maravillosa*," Mrs. Pérez said. She poured a cup of tea and handed it to Rosa. "But also, very tragic. I am so sorry to hear this. Murder is not a good thing to happen at such a happy occasion." She leaned back and crossed herself.

"Thank you," Rosa returned. "It's not how we would have wanted the celebration to end."

Silence descended for a moment as all three carefully sipped their tea.

"How can we help you?" Julio Pérez asked, quickly getting to the point. "I mean, we love to have company and have nice conversations with an interesting young lady like yourself, but you said you had questions for us?"

Rosa folded her hands in her lap. "Yes, well, first of all, I would like to say that I have heard good things about the work you do in Santa Bonita, and I would like to congratulate you on your service."

"Oh?" Mrs. Pérez looked pleased. "What have you heard?"

"That you help immigrants adjust to their new lives in America."

"S*i, si*, we like to do that." Julio Pérez nodded

slowly and then smiled at his wife. "Since coming to America over ten years ago, we have quickly become part of the community at St. Francis and are grateful for how Father Navarro, and especially Sister Evangeline, helped us in the beginning. The sister has a huge heart and so much energy!"

"We think it's important to give back what has been given to us in kindness," Mrs. Pérez said.

Rosa inclined her head. "I understand that you like to focus on assisting single women and young mothers."

"*Si*. It seems there are more of them than ever before coming to us from Mexico," Mr. Pérez said. "They come from faraway places like Guadalajara, and as near as Los Mochis."

"From all over Sinaloa," Mrs. Pérez interjected. "Some come from bad situations, like poverty and bad marriages. Like us, they look for a better life. And they can find it too. They only need a little help."

"What about Alicia Rodriguez?" Rosa asked. "What can you tell me about her?"

Mrs. Pérez pulled back, her face clouding with suspicion. "Why do you ask about her?"

"She's a potential witness to the crime that happened on my wedding day," Rosa said. "And as you know, she works for my cousin Clarence."

"Oh, that's right," Mr. Pérez said. "I'd forgotten the connection."

"As I explained on the phone," Rosa continued, "I'm working with the police as an investigative consultant."

"She's a good girl, our Alicia," Mrs. Pérez said. "She came to us from a bad situation like so many other girls. The young man she was with was very cruel and violent. We counseled her to get right with God and to forgive. Forgiveness is the antidote for a lot of things. You can move on if you can forgive the one who hurt you. Sometimes we don't see the judgment for their actions, not in this life. But God knows, and that is His business."

"Did she ever talk to you about someone named Donald Sussman?" Rosa asked.

Mr. Pérez shared a look with his wife, then said, "We don't know that man personally. But Alicia once mentioned that she did not like Mr. Sussman. I got the feeling that she was scared of him. I don't know why, and she would not say when I asked her."

Rosa felt a sharp pang of concern for Alicia Rodriguez. She hoped that Miguel and his colleagues had tracked the man down. Was it possible he'd go after Alicia? And if so, why?

"Did you work with the immigration authorities to help Alicia get her residence permit here?" Rosa asked.

The question had an immediate effect on both of her hosts. Their facial expressions flattened as they straightened up in their chairs.

"We're not involved in that," Mr. Pérez finally said.

"Oh?" Rosa said with sincere surprise. "I thought that was part of the work you do."

"No, not really." Mrs. Pérez' mouth formed a tight line. "And not in the case of Alicia.

Rosa got the strongest impression that perhaps Alicia's immigrant paperwork wasn't in order.

"I'm not an immigration officer," she said, hoping to reassure them. "That is not my purpose here. I'm only trying to gain information that might lead to the identification of Miss Charlene Winters' killer."

When neither Pérez responded, Rosa tried another tactic. "Is Alicia's job for the Forrester family her first job in America?"

Mr. Pérez shook his head. With notable reluctance, he said, "She first worked in Los Angeles for an actress."

"Julio!" Mrs. Pérez blurted.

"You heard her," Mr. Pérez said. "She works with the police. They're going to find out, anyway."

"Find out what?" Rosa asked.

Mrs. Pérez huffed. "She worked as a cleaner for the dead woman."

"Miss Winters?" Rosa's voice couldn't hide her shock.

"Sí. But only for three months," Mr. Pérez said. "Then she quit."

"Miss Winters," Isabella Pérez crossed herself, "God rest her soul, was not very kind to Alicia. She called her names that I will not repeat and constantly put her down. Alicia already had enough of that in Mexico. She came to us in tears one night and told us bad stories about how Miss Winters threatened her."

"Threatened her how?" Rosa asked. "Do you mean with violence?"

"No..."

Julio Pérez broke in to help his wife out. "Let's just say Miss Winters knew something about Alicia. Something about, you know, possibly her residence status here in America or something like that." He shook his head and threw up his hands with palms facing Rosa. "I don't know about it; I am just saying."

"She is happy with her new job taking care of Julie Forrester," Mrs. Pérez said. "Mr. Forrester treats her well. It is okay to leave it at that, *sí?*"

Rosa expressed her gratitude and did her best to reassure the couple. She didn't know if Alicia was in danger or if she'd jumped a spot on the suspect list, but she knew she needed to speak to the nanny as soon as possible.

24

Rosa had grown up with a father who was an enthusiastic supporter of several sporting activities, but his favorite by far was cricket. Rosa often heard him comment on the latest championship matches at the dinner table, in his study while reading the newspaper, while driving Rosa to visit her friends, while sipping brandy with her mother, and even when they went on holiday to the seaside. Rosa had accompanied him to a few matches as a young girl, but she found it dreadfully boring, much to her father's dismay. What had amazed her as a young girl, however, was the way her father could prattle on about cricket at length while all he ever got from his wife on the subject was a patient nodding of the head or an occasional "Uh-hmm" while she continued about her business.

Baseball was never mentioned unless brought up by a foreigner.

Rosa's first real encounter with the game had been when she was fifteen and newly arrived in Santa Bonita. During the war, her parents had sent her here to stay with her relatives at the Forrester mansion, intending to get her out of harm's way. Britain was at war with Germany, and Rosa's parents' fear of German bombing campaigns proved well founded. The decision to send her to America dramatically changed the course of her life.

As she parked her Corvette in the gravel parking lot at the Santa Bonita baseball fields on the edge of town, Rosa pushed these thoughts aside. It was a beautiful sunny day, and she was glad she had her cat-eye sunglasses.

The crowd was sparse, and she soon spotted Scout and Clarence, along with little Julie, sitting in the top row of the green wooden bleachers that needed a new coat of paint.

"Hi, Rosa!" Julie shouted while fervently chewing on a mouthful of hot dog. There was mustard on her cheek, but she was grinning from ear to ear.

"Hi, Julie," Rosa said as she sat beside the child. "You look like you're having a jolly good time."

The little girl nodded enthusiastically.

"Howdy," Clarence said.

Scout added his hello as he removed his hat and wiped his brow with a white handkerchief. Rosa grinned. It took a while to acclimatize to the California heat.

"So, who are we watching?" Rosa said, looking down at the game that, according to the scoreboard, was in its last inning.

"In the blue, we have the Tigers," Clarence answered. "From south Santa Bonita."

"Alicia is playing for Las Amazonas!" Julie exclaimed as she pointed down at the field. "They are in green." Rosa patted the excited girl on the back. If nothing else, the nanny had done a fine job of winning Julie's affections.

"She's one of their star hitters," Clarence added with a note of pride. He jumped in with his inevitable play-by-play analysis for Scout, who knew virtually nothing of the game. Scout, for his part, seemed fascinated by every aspect of it.

"There's Alicia!" Julie shouted as she pointed her small finger to the player at bat. It took a moment for Rosa to recognize Alicia in her green uniform and hat as she swung the bat as a short warm-up. She was the fourth up as three other runners stood perched on all three bases.

Clarence leaned toward Scout. "Bases are loaded!"

Scout cupped his hands and yelled down to Alicia.

"Bat on!" She didn't seem to hear it, but the people in the seats below did. They stared quizzically over their shoulders, making both Rosa and Julie giggle. "This is bloody excitin' innit, Rosa?" Scout added with a grin.

"O' 'ere it comes now, eh?" Rosa elbowed Scout in the ribs. "The ol' cockney makin' an appearance."

"'Ere now." Scout feigned his complaint at being nudged. "I'm tryin' to enjoy meself."

Alicia was dressed in the team uniform of green button-down shirts, short matching skirts with leather belts buckled at the waist, black cleats with knee-high socks, and a team ball cap on the head, shading the eyes. She poised a bat over her right shoulder, lifted her left foot slightly, and planted it down again, widening her stance as her weight shifted. At the same time, she swiveled her hips to the left, threw her left elbow out, and expertly swung the bat with a force Mickey Mantle would have coveted. There was a resounding crack as wood and stitched cowhide met in a violent encounter. The ball rocketed high in the air over the distant cedar fence that encircled the grounds.

The small crowd erupted in cheers as Alicia dropped her bat and jogged toward first base. She smiled, probably knowing she could take her time.

Clarence and Julie stood and cheered. Clarence cried out, "That is the *most*!"

"Blimey," Scout said, his face flush as he wiped it with his handkerchief again.

Rosa applauded with the rest, but another rather disturbing image captured her mind. Instead of a baseball bat in her hands, she saw Alicia capably wielding a heavy frying pan.

25

A cheer roared from the stands when the Tigers' third batter struck out. Most spectators in the small crowd were there to cheer on Las Amazonas, the "home team." A few moments later, the opposing teams lined up single file across the field in a handshaking ritual while the crowd dispersed from the bleachers.

Scout nudged Rosa's shoulder. "That was a bit of fun, eh? It's always more interesting when one knows one of the players."

"Indeed," Rosa said, her eyes staying on Alicia as the nanny snaked through the lineup on the field below.

"I told you she was one of the best players," Clarence said proudly. "C'mon, let's head down." He scooped Julie into his arms, and Rosa and Scout stepped in behind them.

Alicia spotted them when they reached the field. With a victorious smile on her face, she pranced over. "I am so glad you could make it!"

"Another win!" Clarence said, smiling broadly at Alicia.

Rosa felt he stood a little too close to his nanny and maneuvered herself between them. Would Clarence have hugged the nanny if Rosa herself and Scout hadn't been there? A kiss on the cheek? Politely, she added, "Yes, fine playing, Alicia."

"Thank you, Mrs. Belmonte," Alicia returned demurely.

Julie threw her arms around her nanny's waist. "You were great, Alicia!"

"Hey, *chica*, thank you!" Alicia returned the hug and kissed the girl on the head.

Rosa noted how close the relationship between Julie and her nanny seemed after such a short time. Perhaps it was the inherent need of a little girl for a consistent mother figure which Alicia seemed to fill quite naturally in lieu of Vanessa, who, in Rosa's opinion, was not fulfilling her role. The connection between Alicia, Clarence, and Julie was obviously getting more complicated as time passed. Rosa hoped there would be no more collateral damage—little Julie Forrester had already gone through enough.

"We had them on the run from the beginning," Alicia said, her gaze moving between Julie and Clarence. "They are a good team but no match for Las Amazonas!" She held up her right arm and flexed her bicep.

"I'm going to play for Las Amazonas too," Julie said. She threw up her arm and flexed, mimicking Alicia.

Alicia laughed. "Yes, one day maybe, *chica*."

"That was an impressive stroke," Scout said to Alicia as he mimed swinging a bat in the air.

"It's called a home run," Clarence said with a chuckle. "A stroke doesn't quite seem to describe it."

"Are there many of these women's leagues in amateur baseball?" Scout asked.

"More and more," Alicia said. "I think this one is organized well." The nanny reveled in the high of winning, though her dark eyes flicked a little with anxiety every time she glanced at Rosa.

"I'm wondering if I could have a word with you in private, Alicia," Rosa said.

The smile fell off the young woman's face. "I . . . I came here with the rest of the team in a bus," Alicia said. "They are leaving now." She pointed her chin at a small school bus on the edge of the field. All the women in green were slowly climbing onboard.

"We can give you a ride home, no problem," Clarence offered.

"I have my car here," Rosa said. "I can take her wherever she needs to go. I'm afraid it's police business, so I need to talk to her alone."

"Is this about the murder case?" Clarence asked, a look of concern spreading onto his face.

"It won't take long," Rosa replied.

"Oh, okay," Alicia said. "Uhm, I just need to tell the team's captain." She turned and jogged a few paces toward the bus and then spoke to the person at the end of the line. Rosa watched carefully to ensure Alicia didn't hop on the bus at the last minute, but the nanny seemed too sensible to pull something like that.

"All right then," Clarence said as he took Julie's hand. "We'll see you in a while." He waved at Alicia, and then he, Scout, and Julie started toward the parking lot where the Bel Air was parked.

As Alicia slowly walked back, she stuffed her hands into her pockets and stared nervously at Rosa through long dark lashes.

"My car is over that way too," Rosa said.

Alicia nodded, then said, "Oh wait, I almost forgot I am supposed to take care of all the bats and gloves this week. They are in the dugout. I need to do that before I leave."

"I'll help you," Rosa said, though she wondered what would've happened to the bats and gloves had Alicia hopped the bus like she'd wanted to.

In the Las Amazonas dugout, two large canvas bags had been left on the bench, with several bats, a few balls, and about a dozen leather baseball gloves. So, Alicia hadn't been fibbing about that. In all her excitement, she really had forgotten.

"This equipment belongs to the league," Alicia explained as they stepped into the small covered area.

"I can help," Rosa said. She motioned to a bag. "Shall I start by putting these gloves into this bag?"

"You don't have to help, Mrs. Belmonte."

"I don't mind."

Alicia flashed her a blank look. "Then yes, that's where they go."

As Alicia collected the baseball equipment, she asked, "Why do you want to talk to me alone?"

"There are some loose ends that need to be addressed," Rosa replied.

Alicia hesitated. "Do you know who killed her yet?"

"We have some strong suspicions."

"What are you going to ask me?"

As Alicia fidgeted with the bag's handles, the rosy

blush brought on by exertion and excitement faded to pale. Bases loaded in the last inning, no problem, but after a few minutes alone with Rosa, she looked like she was about to faint.

Rosa stepped closer, waiting to catch Alicia's eyes. Then she asked, "Why didn't you tell the police about your employment with Charlene Winters?"

Alicia looked down, breaking the hold Rosa's eyes had her in and stuffed the large satchel with bats. "I don't know. It didn't seem important."

"Anything that has to do with Miss Winters should be revealed to the police," Rosa said.

"I'm sorry, I didn't mean to hide anything."

"Then why did you?"

Alicia stopped what she was doing and sat down on the bench, looking dejected.

"I like working for Mr. Forrester. He is a good man. And Julie." She took a long, shaky breath, releasing it slowly. "She is such a good girl."

"Julie appears to be fond of you."

Alicia's eyes glistened with tears. "I came from a tough situation in Mexico. And now, I finally found a place where I feel like I belong. Clarence . . . Mr. Forrester . . . is very kind to me." A tear was now rolling down her cheek. "You understand how I dream!" she added dramatically. "You married a Mexican!"

"Yes, I did," Rosa said. Not wanting to go over the

obvious differences in their situations, she continued, "We need to go back to the subject of Miss Winters."

"She treated me very, very badly," Alicia said. "Very rude. She paid me almost nothing, and her apartment was very messy. I had to clean this up!" Alicia threw up her hands. "She made me get groceries for her, and when I returned, she said it was all the wrong things, even though I got what she told me. She called me names. Bad names. Sometimes she would punch my shoulder or even slap my face. I had enough of this in Mexico already, Mrs. Belmonte, I couldn't take it anymore, so I quit." She ran a finger under an eye to stop the tear trail. "I think a lot about what could be, how perfect my life would be if I married Mr. Forrester. Miss Winters was going to ruin it all. She was going to tell the authorities!"

Clearly, Alicia Rodriguez hadn't factored in Aunt Louisa and her formidable will. There was no way on God's green earth that Clarence would've gotten her blessing to marry the nanny. Aunt Louisa had done her best to keep Rosa and Miguel apart when they were younger. And Rosa was merely a niece, not her only son. Removing Clarence from the will wasn't something Rosa would put past her aunt, and she knew Clarence well enough to know that he enjoyed wealth and the leisure it brought. Alicia's hopes were going to be dashed; it was only a matter of time.

"And that's the reason you held back that information." It was more of a statement than a question, as Rosa was certain it could be viewed as a motive.

Alicia ran a sleeve under her nose as she nodded. "Yes."

"Did you have any contact with Miss Winters after you left her employ?" Rosa asked.

"Only at your wedding," Alicia said sadly. "I thought I was free of her. I tried to ignore her, but she wouldn't leave me alone."

"She wanted you to work for her again?" Rosa asked incredulously.

"No. She wanted me to quit working for Mr. Forrester."

Alicia's answer was an even bigger surprise. "Why would she want that?"

"I am not sure." Alicia faced Rosa, narrowing her watery eyes on her. "But I think it has something to do with you. She didn't like that you were going to marry Mr. Belmonte."

Rosa grunted. Charlene Winters was so jealous of Rosa that she couldn't stand to see any happiness come to the Forrester house. "I saw you having a heated discussion with Miss Winters at the reception party. Beside the pool."

"You saw?"

"Yes, is that what you were arguing about? Your employment at the Forrester mansion?"

"She was a terrible woman, Mrs. Belmonte. I decided I won't let her push me around anymore. And then I saw her ignoring her date, Mr. Brummel. Instead, she was flirting with Detective Belmonte! I'm sorry, but I saw it happen."

"Yes, I saw it too," Rosa said. "But she couldn't just demand that you quit your job. She had no right to do that."

Alicia stood and put her hands on the wire mesh that separated the dugout from the rest of the field. "She demanded that I quit."

As Rosa stared at the back of Alicia Rodriguez, she recalled her conversation with the Pérezes and her own hunch that things weren't always run by the book.

"Miss Winters didn't want you to work for Mr. Forrester, but she was threatening you with something else as well, wasn't she?"

Alicia stiffened, her fingers white-knuckling as she gripped the mesh.

"You're in America illegally, aren't you?"

It was like all life energy suddenly drained out of Alicia. Her shoulders sagged as she leaned into the mesh, and one hand went to her mouth, stifling a sob.

"I'm not with immigration authorities, Alicia,"

Rosa said quietly. "That's not why I'm here. You can trust me. Things can be worked out."

"I . . . can't go back." Alicia turned around, keeping her hands behind her as she leaned on the wire. Her eyes were red, and her mouth had turned into a hard line.

"I'm afraid I need to ask you again, Alicia," Rosa started. "Where were you when Charlene was killed?"

"I was giving Julie cake." Alicia froze, her eyes darting as she registered her misstep. "I mean, I was in the restroom. I think something I ate was not right in my stomach."

Rosa asked carefully. "Were you with Julie or in the restroom?"

"The restroom."

"Are you certain, Alicia? We have a witness who was also in the restroom at that time, and she swears she was alone." Rosa held Alicia's gaze. Doris Brinkley's testimony was weak, but Alicia didn't know that.

"I meant I was with Julie. We were on our way to the restroom. She still needs help."

Alicia placed the heavy end of a bat on the bench and leaned on it with her hand on the end of the handle.

"You know what I think, Alicia?" Rosa began. "I think you were on your way to a restroom, but not the public one in the foyer, and not with Julie beside you. I think you saw Miss Winters head through the door by the kitchen and knew that the only reason she'd go through there was because of the private restroom at the back. I think you left the reception hall through the main doors, circled through the foyer, and headed down the adjoining hall that leads to the kitchen. I believe you wanted to confront Miss Winters. I imagine she laughed at you, perhaps even pushed you away, making you feel humiliated and belittled. I don't think you meant to kill her, Alicia, but in your rage, you picked up a discarded frying pan sitting within reach and smashed it against Miss Winters' head. Much like you hit a ball with the bat to get a home run."

"You're right. I didn't mean to kill her!"

Rosa gaped at Alicia, who immediately slapped her palm over her mouth. Rosa said carefully, "Tell me what happened."

"Miss Winters purposely bumped into me at the reception," Alicia said with a hardened voice. "Causing me to spill the drinks just to embarrass me again."

Alicia lifted the bat and let it drop back onto the bench with a loud bumping sound. "When I stopped working for her and came here, I thought I'd never see her again. I couldn't believe it when she showed up for your rehearsal party."

Rosa nodded, remembering the altercation she'd witnessed between them.

"When she left the hall through the kitchen door . . ." Alicia glanced at Rosa, a dead look in her eyes. "I knew where she was going. I attend St. Francis Church. I help clean it for extra money. I *clean* that restroom."

"So, you followed her?"

"Yes. I followed her. I waited in the hallway for her. That vain woman was in there *forever*. I finally knocked on the door to get her out. When she saw me standing there, she pushed me, just like you said. I fell to the ground, and she laughed. She laughed at me! So yes, I played baseball with her head. But I didn't mean to kill her, Mrs. Belmonte. I swear I didn't."

Rosa stepped closer, hoping to calm the girl. "It's not over for you, Alicia. We can work with the authorities."

"No! They will send me back to Mexico! I will not go back."

Rosa flinched as Alicia suddenly brought the end of the bat down on the bench with a loud bang. "I'm so sorry," Alicia said. Her eyes welled up again, but this time her gaze intensified with a look of resolve. Gripping the bat with both hands, she raised it over her right shoulder, ready to swing.

Instinctively, Rosa lunged and shoved her forearm into Alicia's left elbow, throwing her off balance. This effort caused Alicia to spin to the right, allowing Rosa to grab the heavy end of the bat with her right hand while encircling the woman's throat with her left arm.

Alicia immediately dropped the bat and collapsed to her knees.

"Alicia," Rosa started as she helped the girl off the ground, "You have to go to the police."

Alicia sat on the bench with an air of defeat. "I didn't put her in that trolley."

Rosa stared back. "You didn't?"

"No." With round glassy eyes, Alicia continued, "That was so confusing for me, Mrs. Belmonte. I hit Miss Winters, and she fell to the floor. She was moaning and even swore a little, so that's how I knew she was alive. I was so shocked at what I'd done, I dropped the frying pan and ran."

Was Alicia Rodriguez telling the truth? Clearly, she could wield a heavy frying pan, but Rosa had always found it difficult to imagine her successfully hiding a body in a trolley.

"Why didn't you say something?" Rosa asked.

"Why bother? I still hit her. I'm the reason she's dead."

If Charlene was still alive after Alicia hit her, then it was true that the killer had taken advantage of the actress's weakened state to finish her off.

"Alicia," Rosa started, "did you see anyone in the foyer when you ran away?"

"I don't know." Alicia pushed tears off her cheek. "I can't remember."

"Try," Rosa said. "Think back to that time. You were furious at Miss Winters, and without thinking it through, you picked up a frying pan and hit her. She fell to the ground, and you dropped the frying pan."

"Oh, Mrs. Belmonte! It makes me sick to think about it!"

"Please, Alicia. This is important." Rosa squatted to look the nanny in the eye. "You raced out of the kitchen, down the adjoining hallway, through the foyer, and back to the reception hall. Did you see anyone? Perhaps in your peripheral vision?"

Alicia stared blankly ahead in thought, her eyes darting about as if her mind was racing. Then, they lit up. She locked her gaze on Rosa. "I did see someone. Standing behind the potted plant. I barely registered him in my rush."

"Who was it, Alicia?"

The nanny locked her gaze on Rosa. "Mr. Sussman."

26

With a measure of urgency, Rosa drove toward the police department. Alicia held on to the passenger side handgrip with a look of consternation on her face. When Rosa hit a curb, Alicia called out, "Mrs. Belmonte!"

"Do forgive me, Alicia," Rosa returned. "It's rather important that I relay this information to the police."

When Donald Sussman had dodged Rosa and Miguel at the winery, she'd thought it was because of his alleged connection to communist machinations, but was he a murderer as well? Despite the all-points bulletin put out to find him, Mr. Sussman remained elusive, and Rosa wouldn't be surprised if the man had somehow made it back to Argentina.

And then, as if her thoughts had conjured the man up, there he was, standing outside an apartment building with a young woman. Rosa made a sharp turn into a parking stall and came to a sudden stop.

Alicia put both hands on the dash to brace herself. "Mrs. Belmonte!"

Rosa kept her sights on Donald Sussman and the woman who were heading to the entrance of the building. Rosa squinted as she stared at the woman. "Doris Brinkley!"

"Pardon?" Alicia said, looking perplexed.

"Alicia, I need you to do me a favor," Rosa said as she dug through her purse for a few coins. "It's very important. See that telephone booth? I need you to call the police."

Alicia blanched. "The police?"

Rosa took Alicia's hand and forced the coins into her fist. "Yes. Ask for Detective Belmonte and tell him that Mr. Sussman is the killer, that I'm with him at the Palm Grove Apartments on Fifth Avenue, and that we're at Miss Doris Brinkley's place." Staring intensely into the nanny's eyes, she added, "Can you do that?"

Alicia nodded. "Yes, ma'am. Then what should I do?"

"Take a taxi home." Rosa removed a couple of bills from her wallet and handed them to Alicia. "I'll see you again later."

As Alicia made the call, Rosa headed to the apartment building. Had Mr. Sussman been hiding out with

Miss Brinkley this whole time? Had the actress really been getting sick in the church restrooms, or had she been involved in the murder of Charlene Winters?

The front door of the apartment building was unlocked, and Rosa checked for Miss Brinkley's apartment number on the directory in the foyer. Number 105.

The building had three floors, but fortunately, Miss Brinkley's apartment was on the first. When Rosa reached the door, she could hear voices, one male and one female. Rosa pressed her ear against the door, hoping to make out what was being said, but she could only catch phrases.

"Need to leave."

"I'm packing!"

"Should've gone yesterday."

They were getting ready to leave town. To keep them from taking off, Rosa knocked. The voices stopped, and after the sound of shuffling—Mr. Sussman, no doubt trying to hide—the door opened a crack, and Miss Brinkley stared out.

"Mrs. Belmonte?" she said with surprise in her voice. "What are you doing here?"

"I was in the neighborhood and thought I'd drop in." Taking advantage of Miss Brinkley's momentary stupefaction, Rosa casually crossed the threshold.

"Oh, wait," Miss Brinkley said. "I'm not really

prepared for visitors." She smirked with feigned self-deprecation. "I'm such a poor housekeeper."

"I don't mind," Rosa said. "I'm not much better. I wouldn't mind a cup of tea if you have it."

Rosa knew she was being rude and brash, but she also knew Miss Brinkley was harboring a killer. Miguel was sure to be on his way, and she only had to inconvenience the actress and the fugitive for a short while.

"I'm afraid I don't have any tea. Nor coffee or any beverages," Miss Brinkley said stiffly.

"I see," Rosa said. "What about a glass of water?" She lowered herself onto an armchair. "I'm still not used to this California heat, and I'm feeling flushed."

Miss Brinkley's lips tightened. Her eyes flashed with indecision until she finally relented. "Of course, I have water."

Miss Brinkley disappeared into the small kitchen, and the sound of running water immediately followed. Rosa scanned her surroundings as she waited. The living room had dated furnishings, was untidy, and in disarray: discarded coats, gloves, hats, old mail, and half-drunk cups of coffee. Miss Brinkley was comfortable in disorder and discord. Rosa guessed that the closed door in the hallway led to the bedroom and that Mr. Sussman was pressed against it. Or had he scampered out the window and down the fire escape?

No. Mr. Sussman was the type of man who

wouldn't consider a woman a threat. At best, he'd wait her out. At worst, he'd force her hand.

Miss Brinkley returned with a glass of water, and Rosa accepted it with thanks. But she decided not to take a drink. She didn't trust Miss Brinkley, and an impromptu poisoning plot wasn't out of the question. Instead, she said, "I see you've packed. Are you going somewhere?"

"I am, Mrs. Belmonte. Which is why I'm afraid I don't have time to visit. I'm about to leave for LA. I have an audition tonight, so I really must be going."

"Miss Brinkley, what is your association with Donald Sussman?"

Doris Brinkley's false eyelashes batted. "What do you mean? I-I have no association."

"Mr. Sussman hasn't approached you about the New National Theater Coalition? It's a cover for communist propaganda and recruitment. Perhaps he wanted you to be an influencer in Hollywood for his cause?"

"N-no. Why would he? I'm a nobody in the industry."

"You're being too humble, Miss Brinkley," Rosa said. "I've heard you might be in the running to replace Miss Winters in her show."

It was a bluff, but Rosa had learned that appealing to a suspect's ego was often effective.

Miss Brinkley took the bait, her countenance softening. "You have? Where did you hear that?"

"Oh, let me see. I think I read about it in one of the entertainment magazines. An opinion piece, I believe. Your name was suggested as the replacement. Perhaps Mr. Sussman has offered to help you climb the so-called ladder? In exchange for certain discretions?"

Miss Brinkley's look tightened. "I don't know what you mean."

"You do know that Mr. Sussman is under suspicion for communist activities, including recruitment. And the police now believe he killed Miss Winters."

Miss Brinkley blanched as her knees appeared to give out. She braced herself against the arm of the sofa.

"No. He didn't do that. It was that Mexican nanny." Miss Brinkley glared at Rosa. "The one that works for your cousin."

Rosa cocked her head. "And how would you know that, Miss Brinkley? You told the police you were ill in the church restrooms. Unless . . ."

"No! I was in the restroom. I had nothing to do with Charlene's death. Mr. Suss—"

Mr. Sussman's thundering voice followed the sound of a door being thrown open and smacking the wall. "That's enough, Doris! You bumbling idiot!"

Like an angry hippo, Donald Sussman barrelled

down the hallway, a revolver pointed in their direction. "The both of you, stay where you are!"

"Donald—" Miss Brinkley started. "She had me riled up!"

"For the love of Pete, shut your mouth! I need to think."

Miss Brinkley's lips tightened as she narrowed her eyes at the man. "Let's just tie her up and go," she said. "No one knows she's here."

"It's strange the police aren't pounding on the door." Donald Sussman stared at Rosa. "Are you really so stupid as to come here alone?"

Alicia had called the police, hadn't she? Rosa had depended on the girl's proven competence, but had she misplaced her trust?

She hoped not.

Rosa forced herself to look remorseful. "I just happened to see you pull up and followed you in. I didn't think it through, I guess."

Doris Brinkley sprang to her feet and raced to the kitchen. "I have some twine!"

Mr. Sussman set his steely gaze on Rosa. "And why shouldn't I just kill you?"

"Well, for one thing," Rosa said, forcing a calm demeanor, "California law for murder is capital punishment."

"I think we both know I'd be down for that

anyway."

"So, you're admitting to killing Charlene Winters?"

Donald Sussman shrugged. "It was an opportunity of convenience. I saw Charlene enter the kitchen and was waiting around for her to come out. We needed to talk, you see.

"About the New National Theater Coalition?"

"She was trying to blackmail me. Threatened to expose me if I didn't get her the parts she wanted." He threw his free hand into the air. "Like I was a miracle worker. She had looks, but her acting skills were just so-so."

"So, you followed her into the kitchen?" Rosa prompted.

"I saw the Mexican nanny run from the kitchen like it was on fire and about to explode. I was curious, so I went in."

"And you found Charlene Winters knocked out?"

Mr. Sussman chuckled. "You're good. Yeah, but she was coming to. I saw the frying pan on the floor and gave her another whack. Finished the job, and good riddance, I say."

"And you put the frying pan in the dishwasher?"

"I was kinda pressed for time. The kitchen workers would come back at any moment, and I had to hurry. I shoulda used a towel or something to keep my fingerprints off the thing, then that Mexican gal would've gone down for the deed. But I didn't, and now my prints were on it. I tossed it in that dang dishwasher and pushed the 'On' button, hoping for the best. I barely dragged Charlene into the trolley room before the song ended and the workers came in. The thing is, I put her in one of the trolleys in the back. Beats me why they used that one to bring out the dessert."

"The other trolleys had broken wheels," Rosa explained. From the corner of her eye, she saw Miss Brinkley looking out of the kitchen doorway. Returning her focus to Mr. Sussman, she said, "Bad luck for you."

"Yeah, well, now it's bad luck for you, Mrs. Belmonte. Since I confessed, I must kill you."

Mr. Sussman steadied his aim. Rosa kept her gaze on him, holding his attention.

"Now!" Rosa shouted, then ducked just as the gun blast went off. This was followed by the bang of a heavy body hitting the floor.

Doris Brinkley dropped the frying pan she'd just wielded against Mr. Sussman's head.

In the distance, Rosa registered the sound of police car sirens. She held Miss Brinkley's gaze. The woman had successfully duped a con artist. "You're a good actress, Miss Brinkley."

"Thank you, Mrs. Belmonte," Doris Brinkley said with a grin. "That means a lot!"

27

Rosa hadn't had a chance to appreciate her new home's back garden—or "yard" as the Americans liked to call it. Miguel didn't have much of a green thumb, so after a bit of cajoling, he realized the benefits of hiring the Forrester gardener, Bernardo Diaz, to come and clean it up a bit. Mr. Diaz did a fine job trimming the hedges and cutting the lawn and had several suggestions for flower beds along the fence line.

The yard had turned out so nicely that Rosa was eager to host her first garden party. She and Miguel set up a table and nine chairs, strung lights between the trees, and lit several candles.

When it came to the food, Rosa had to admit defeat. She'd never learned her way around a kitchen except for how to make toast and tea. Carlotta came to her rescue. After a delightful honeymoon, Carlotta and Bill were an embarrassment of affection, and to those in the know, the new Mrs. Sanchez was glowing.

"I'll just put a roast in the oven with potatoes and carrots," she'd said, "and I'll bake a chocolate cake. All you'll have to do, Rosa, is a salad."

Rosa didn't want to admit to her new sister-in-law that she didn't even know how to correctly assemble one, but after a short tutorial from Señora Gomez, she'd tossed a green salad like the best of them.

Bill and Carlotta arrived with the roast beef and dessert as promised. Rosa and Miguel's other guests were Clarence, Gloria and Jake, Jake's sister, Barbara, who'd just moved to Santa Bonita from Oregon, and Scout, who was due to return to England the next day. The thought of saying goodbye to her brother made Rosa's chest squeeze with sadness, so with determination, she forced her emotions aside to be dealt with in the morning.

"Your aunt and grandmother aren't coming?" Carlotta asked as she cut the roast in Rosa's small kitchen.

"Grandma Sally is watching Julie," Rosa said. "And Aunt Louisa is on a date." Her aunt had finally swallowed her pride and made the ranch manager a happier man.

"Roundtree is a fine chap," Scout said, stepping inside in time to catch the end of the conversation. "I did enjoy the day we spent on his ranch. I'm almost a fan of the western saddle," he added with his trademark toothy grin. "Almost. Now, where might I find the loo? Ah, never mind. I see it."

The house was so small that one didn't need directions to find anything, but Rosa had learned to embrace it as quaint.

Miguel was in the backyard entertaining the other guests. Rosa dished the potatoes and carrots into a bowl —there was enough to feed twice as many people as were present—and removed her salad from the refrigerator.

It'd been two weeks since the arrest of Donald Sussman. Doris Brinkley vowed she hadn't known Mr. Sussman was in trouble with the law and was only housing him at her apartment as a favor, with hopes he'd return it by helping her get acting work.

"He slept on the couch; I promise."

After hearing his confessions while his gun was leveled at Rosa, Miss Brinkley had been clever enough to know she needed to act.

"Or get dragged into his dirty business, and I wasn't going to jail for that slimeball."

She agreed to testify against him and was rather

gleeful about the attention. The notoriety seemed to have launched her into the spotlight. Rosa had seen an announcement in the TV guide that Miss Brinkley had gotten a role on *As the World Turns*.

The police wanted Alicia Rodriguez for assault, causing bodily harm. Nobody had seen or heard from her after she'd made that phone call to the police. Rosa suspected she'd taken the money she'd been given for a taxi and hopped a bus out of town. Julio and Isabella Pérez insisted that they never heard from Alicia, but Rosa, for one, would not press them about it. Alicia was a bright and resourceful girl and had probably found her way to another couple in the southern states who made it their mission to help girls like her.

"I brought a bottle of wine," Gloria said once Rosa and Carlotta had set the food on the table. She laughed. "I'm sure Mom won't miss it from her collection."

Rosa wasn't sure of that, but who was she to tell Gloria differently? Jake Wilson sat beside Gloria with his sister Barbara on his other side. Rosa was pleased to see how attentive he was to Gloria, even while sharing his attention with everyone else. She wouldn't be surprised if another wedding announcement was on the horizon.

Clarence had been entrenched in melancholy and

self-pity since Alicia's departure, proving to everyone that he'd had stronger feelings for her than he had liked to admit. Like Grandma Sally, Rosa hoped he'd meet someone nice—and without a criminal record—to build a life with.

Rosa's eyes darted to Barbara Wilson. Her move to Santa Bonita had come at a fortuitous time. Rosa had had the pleasure of meeting her before this party, and in truth, Barbara had been a driving impetus in her decision to throw the party. She seemed very *nice* and *law-abiding* and, just as importantly, single. Her wish that Clarence would snap out of his somber mood and notice Barbara seemed to be granted. Clarence gazed unabashedly in Barbara's direction.

Miguel stood with a glass in hand when the cake was brought out. "If I could have everyone's attention, I'd like to make a toast."

Rosa gazed at Miguel with his black hair styled in a ducktail over his forehead and his dark eyes twinkling, and her heart warmed. She returned his smile, and subconsciously her fingers reached for the pearl-cluster earrings clipped to her ears.

"To the health and prosperity of our enjoined families, the Belmontes, Forresters, and Reeds." Rosa glanced across the table at Scout and smiled.

Miguel continued with a nod to the Wilson siblings. "And to friends. Cheers."

A round of "cheers" went up as everyone tipped glasses before drinking.

Rosa stared at her husband as he remained standing.

"Is there more, darling?" she asked.

"Just one thing more," Miguel said, holding her gaze. "To my beautiful wife, Rosa Reed Belmonte, my one and only true love. Thank you for coming back for me."

Rosa grinned as Miguel chuckled.

"And for being willing to marry me, not once, but twice. I love you and look forward to many happy years at your side."

Rosa's eyes burned with tears. She stood, then stepped into Miguel's embrace. "Hear, hear," she said, then kissed him.

Don't miss the next Ginger Gold Mystery
MURDER IN FRANCE

Murder is so *sang-froid*!

When the Reed family—temporarily exiled to France—was once again safe, Ginger decides to turn the event into a much needed holiday. And the absolute cake was Ginger's reunion with her American friend Haley Higgins, who is working in France on a practicum to become a lady doctor.

Ginger celebrates the happy reunion by throwing a party at their villa in Paris, but the joyous activities are halted when a body is discovered. Like old times, Ginger puts her detective skills to work while Haley provides her forensic knowledge. As party guests continue to become more suspicious and worthy suspects, Ginger's own past is soon on trial.

Has a long-ago, war-time "error" resurfaced to steal more than Ginger's *joie de vivre*?

Buy on Amazon or read FREE with a Kindle Unlimited Subscription!

Rosa & Miguel's Wartime Romance is a BONUS short story exclusively for Lee's newsletter subscribers.

Subscribe Now!
https://dl.bookfunnel.com/8n1wooe6rl

MORE FROM LEE STRAUSS

On AMAZON

THE ROSA REED MYSTERIES

(1950s cozy historical)

Murder at High Tide

Murder on the Boardwalk

Murder at the Bomb Shelter

Murder on Location

Murder and Rock 'n Roll

Murder at the Races

Murder at the Dude Ranch

Murder in London

Murder at the Fiesta

Murder at the Weddings

GINGER GOLD MYSTERY SERIES (cozy 1920s historical)

Cozy. Charming. Filled with Bright Young Things. This Jazz Age murder mystery will entertain and delight you with its 1920s flair and pizzazz!

Murder on the SS Rosa

Murder at Hartigan House

Murder at Bray Manor

Murder at Feathers & Flair

Murder at the Mortuary

Murder at Kensington Gardens

Murder at St. George's Church

The Wedding of Ginger & Basil

Murder Aboard the Flying Scotsman

Murder at the Boat Club

Murder on Eaton Square

Murder by Plum Pudding

Murder on Fleet Street

Murder at Brighton Beach

Murder in Hyde Park

Murder at the Royal Albert Hall

Murder in Belgravia

Murder on Mallowan Court

Murder at the Savoy

Murder at the Circus

Murder in France

Murder at Yuletide

LADY GOLD INVESTIGATES (Ginger Gold companion short stories)

Volume 1

Volume 2

Volume 3

Volume 4

HIGGINS & HAWKE MYSTERY SERIES (cozy 1930s historical)

The 1930s meets Rizzoli & Isles in this friendship depression era cozy mystery series.

Death at the Tavern

Death on the Tower

Death on Hanover

Death by Dancing

A NURSERY RHYME MYSTERY SERIES(mystery/sci fi)

Marlow finds himself teamed up with intelligent and savvy Sage Farrell, a girl so far out of his league he feels blinded in her presence - literally - damned glasses! Together they work to find the identity of @gingerbreadman. Can they stop the killer before he strikes again?

Gingerbread Man

Life Is but a Dream

Hickory Dickory Dock

Twinkle Little Star

LIGHT & LOVE (sweet romance)

Set in the dazzling charm of Europe, follow Katja, Gabriella, Eva, Anna and Belle as they find strength, hope and love.

Love Song

Your Love is Sweet

In Light of Us

Lying in Starlight

PLAYING WITH MATCHES (WW2 history/romance)

A sobering but hopeful journey about how one young German boy copes with the war and propaganda. Based on true events.

A Piece of Blue String (companion short story)

THE CLOCKWISE COLLECTION (YA time travel romance)

Casey Donovan has issues: hair, height and uncontrollable trips to the 19th century! And now this ~ she's accidentally taken Nate Mackenzie, the cutest boy in the school, back in time. Awkward.

Clockwise

Clockwiser

Like Clockwork

Counter Clockwise

Clockwork Crazy

Clocked (companion novella)

Standalones

Seaweed

Love, Tink

ROSA & MIGUEL'S WARTIME ROMANCE

PREQUEL - EXCERPT

Rosa Reed first laid eyes on Miguel Belmonte on the fourteenth day of February in 1945. She was a senior attending a high school dance, and he a soldier who played in the band.

She'd been dancing with her date, Tom Hawkins, a short, stalky boy with pink skin and an outbreak of acne, but her gaze continued to latch onto the bronze-skinned singer, with dark crew-cut hair, looking very dapper in a black suit.

In a life-changing moment, their eyes locked. Despite the fact that she stared at the singer over the shoulder of her date, she couldn't help the bolt of electricity that shot through her, and when the singer smiled—and those dimples appeared—heavens, her knees almost gave out!

"Rosa?"

Tom's worried voice brought her back to reality. "Are you okay? You went a little limp there. Do you feel faint? It is mighty hot in here." Tom released Rosa's hand to tug at his tie. "Do you want to get some air?"

Rosa felt a surge of alarm. Invitations to step outside the gymnasium were often euphemisms to get fresh.

In desperation she searched for her best friend Nancy Davidson—her best *American* friend, that was. Vivien Eveleigh claimed the position of *best* friend back in London, and Rosa missed her. Nancy made for a sufficient substitute. A pretty girl with honey-blond hair, Nancy, fortunately, was no longer dancing, and was sitting alone.

"I think I'll visit the ladies, Tom, if you don't mind."

He looked momentarily put out, then shrugged. "Suit yourself." He joined a group of lads—boys—at the punch table, and joined in with their raucous laughter. Rosa didn't want to know what they were joking about, or at whose expense.

Nancy understood Rosa's plight as she wasn't entirely pleased with her fellow either. "If only you and I could dance with each other."

"One can't very well go to a dance without a date, though," Rosa said.

Nancy laughed. "*One* can't."

Rosa rolled her eyes. Even after four years of living in America, her Englishness still manifested when she was distracted.

And tonight's distraction was the attractive lead singer in the band, and shockingly, he seemed to have sought her face out too.

Nancy had seen the exchange and gave Rosa a firm nudge. "No way, José. I know he's cute, but he's from the wrong side of the tracks. Your aunt would have a conniption."

Nancy wasn't wrong about that. Aunt Louisa had very high standards, as one who was lady of Forrester mansion, might.

"I'm only looking!"

Nancy harrumphed. "As long as it stays that way."

Continue reading >>>

Subscribe Now!

ABOUT THE AUTHORS

Lee Strauss is a USA TODAY bestselling author of The Ginger Gold Mysteries series, The Higgins & Hawke Mystery series, The Rosa Reed Mystery series (cozy historical mysteries), A Nursery Rhyme Mystery series (mystery suspense), The Light & Love series (sweet romance), The Clockwise Collection (YA time travel romance), and young adult historical fiction with over a million books read. She has titles published in German and French, and a growing audio library.

When Lee's not writing or reading she likes to cycle, hike, and stare at the ocean. She loves to drink caffè lattes and red wines in exotic places, and eat dark chocolate anywhere.

Norm Strauss is a singer-songwriter and performing artist who's seen the stage of The Voice of Germany. He now works with his wife Lee Strauss as a writer and publisher.

For more info on books by Lee Strauss and her social media links, visit leestraussbooks.com. To make sure you don't miss the next new release, be sure to sign up for her readers' list!

Discuss the books, ask questions, share your opinions. Fun giveaways! Join the Lee Strauss Readers' Group on Facebook for more info.

Did you know you can follow your favourite authors on Bookbub? If you subscribe to Bookbub — (and if you don't, why don't you? - They'll send you daily emails alerting you to sales and new releases on just the kind of books you like to read!) — follow me to make sure you don't miss the next Ginger Gold Mystery!

www.leestraussbooks.com
leestraussbooks@gmail.com

Printed in Poland
by Amazon Fulfillment
Poland Sp. z o.o., Wrocław

32616966R00138